THE SCANDAL AT 23 MOUNT STREET

An Angela Marchmont Mystery Book 9

CLARA BENSON

MOUNT
STREET
PRESS

MOUNT
STREET
PRESS

Copyright

ClaraBenson.com

Cover design by Shayne Rutherford at
wickedgoodbookcovers.com

Interior Design & Typesetting by Ampersand Book Interiors
ampersandbookinteriors.com

CHAPTER ONE

I T WAS AN ordinary sort of week to begin with. November had set in, and with it a series of dull, overcast days that seemed deliberately calculated to cast a pall over everyone's mood—not least that of Mrs. Angela Marchmont, who, owing to one or two circumstances that could not have been foreseen, found herself stuck at home for several days with nothing to do. The previous Saturday she had been due to visit some friends, but the sudden death of the host's great-aunt had put paid to that. On Monday she had been engaged to dine with an old friend whom she had not seen in some years, but this had had to be postponed when Eva's husband fell ill (had Eva been unwell herself, she would have dragged herself up to London come what may, she assured Angela, but Harold was simply unable to look after himself and could not do without her). In addition to this, Angela's maid, Marthe, was fretting over news of her mother in France, who was prone to depressive fits and had shut herself in her bedroom, vowing never to come out again. Naturally, Angela could not refuse Marthe's request to take a few days' leave to visit her family, but the seasonal gloom had affected her spirits and she was forced to exercise all her good sense in order to suppress the irrational suspicion that everyone had suddenly decided in concert to cause her inconvenience.

Had she known what was about to befall her, Angela might have followed Marthe's mother's example and hidden herself away somewhere, that it might all be avoided, for despite all her best efforts, her life was about to be thrown into the spotlight in the most unwelcome way. In recent years, her involvement in several famous and sensational murder cases had given her a certain amount of celebrity, and although she had never actively sought fame, she had learned to tolerate it and even enjoy it with distant amusement. Still, for the most part she preferred to live privately—for even the best of us have secrets we do not wish to share with the world—and so, had she known that she was about to become the most notorious woman in Britain, and that all her carefully-constructed walls were about to be brought down and her personal actions be exposed to the full, disapproving glare of public judgment, she might well have acted differently that day and saved herself one worry, at least. Of course, like anyone else, Angela had made her fair share of mistakes in life, and if she had a particular fault it was a complacent—perhaps bordering on self-satisfied—belief that she could bury those mistakes, and thus never have to account for them, merely by pretending that they had never happened. Nonetheless, while tea-shops and public houses buzzed with the story and every man and his wife pored over the morning newspaper, eager for each new development in the case, her many well-wishers did tend to agree that it was rather harsh on her to have to pay for her sins *all* at once. That was the nature of justice, however: it pressed on blindly, oblivious to the effect it might have on those in its path as it pursued its ultimate ends. Long after the event, Angela could not help but torment herself, wondering how things might have turned out had she not made the choices she did, but each time she was forced to the inescapable conclusion that had things been otherwise she would most likely be dead herself now, her name a nine days' wonder in the newspapers, soon to be forgotten. Had she done right, though, in accepting the favour offered her and agreeing to that silent bargain which exchanged her life for that of another, however wicked he had proved to be? She did not know, although her guilty conscience would whisper the answer in her ear for a long time to come.

All this was still in the future, however, and far from Angela's mind on Wednesday, as she returned to her flat in Mount Street after a short trip to Regent Street to buy a gift for a friend. To add insult to the injuries of the week, she had given her driver, William, the afternoon off, whereupon it had immediately begun to rain. It started as a mere drizzle, and so she set off boldly on her quest without an umbrella, but by the time she was ready to return, the drizzle had become a deluge and Angela was forced to take a taxi home. The cab drew up opposite the flat and she jumped out and hurried across the road as fast as she could before her parcels got wet. At the outer door of the building she fumbled in her handbag for her keys, but in her haste dropped them in a puddle. Uttering an exclamation of impatience, she was about to bend down and retrieve them when she was forestalled by a man who had been standing in the shelter of the doorway, and who hastened forward to pick them up for her. As she took them from him she caught sight of a pair of deep blue eyes and started in surprise. Down went the keys into the puddle again, this time joined by the parcels.

'Bother!' she exclaimed involuntarily.

'I think they'll be all right,' said Edgar Valencourt, examining one of the unfortunate packages. 'Look, this one's only a little bit wet at the end.'

'I was *not* referring to the parcels,' said Angela, whose heart had set up the most ridiculous flutter.

'Well, that's a fine welcome, I must say,' he said.

'What on earth are you doing here?' she hissed, glancing about, for it did not do to chat idly to wanted criminals in a Mayfair street. 'You said you wouldn't do this.'

'Yes, I did, didn't I?' he said. 'I don't know why you persist in believing me.'

'Nor do I,' she said dryly. She was privately aghast at how her spirits had soared at the sight of him, but there was no use in struggling against it, for there he was, just as she remembered him, smiling as though he were genuinely happy to see her, and try as she might she was unable to arrange her features into the disapproving frown that was required in the circumstances, but could manage only a smile in return.

'That's better,' he said. 'A cross face doesn't suit you.'

'Ought you to be here?' she said. 'Are you safe?'

'As safe as anywhere.'

'Well, I suppose you'd better come in,' she said after a moment. 'This weather is filthy.'

'I knew you wouldn't leave me out in the rain,' he said.

Upstairs, Marthe was bustling about in preparation for her imminent departure. Her eyes gleamed briefly when she saw Valencourt, but her training held good and she said nothing.

'Marthe, you remember Mr.—' said Angela, and hesitated. 'By the way, what are you calling yourself this week?' she inquired sweetly.

'Smart will do,' he said.

'Mr. Smart, then.'

'But of course,' said Marthe. '*Bonjour, monsieur.*'

'I don't know how you keep up with all these names of yours,' said Angela. Her eye fell on an enormous display of white and pink lilies that stood on a nearby table and filled the air with a delicate scent. 'Have these just arrived, Marthe?' she said. 'Who sent them?'

'M. Etheridge,' said Marthe. 'They came an hour ago.'

'Oh, how kind of him,' said Angela. 'I must send him a note of thanks.'

'Mr. Etheridge?' said Valencourt, after Marthe had retired discreetly.

Angela darted him a wicked glance.

'He lives in the flat downstairs, but he has a place in Surrey with a hothouse. He likes to send me flowers sometimes,' she said.

'I see.'

'He's a darling,' said Angela.

'I'm sure he is,' said Valencourt, not taking his eyes off her. Angela relented.

'I think he's about eighty-four,' she said.

'Then he ought to know better, at his age,' said Valencourt. He moved a little closer to her and she retreated slightly. There was a pause. At that moment the telephone-bell rang, rather to Angela's relief. Marthe answered it.

'It is Mrs. Jameson,' she said.

'Do you mind awfully?' said Angela, and took the instrument without waiting for a reply from him. She was on the telephone for some little time—without, probably, saying anything that made much sense, for her mind was elsewhere—and when she finally hung up she turned to find Edgar Valencourt and Marthe talking in French like old friends about a place in France they both knew well. Marthe bobbed and scurried away immediately when she saw her mistress's face.

'That was Kathie Jameson,' said Angela. 'She's a sort of relation of mine. You might recognize the name. A couple of weeks ago she married Inspector Jameson. You know, from Scotland Yard.'

'How splendid. I hope they'll be very happy,' said Valencourt politely.

'I'm sure they will,' said Angela. For some reason she was feeling a little giddy, and the mischief had come upon her, so she beamed angelically and said, 'You can't imagine what a comfort it will be to have a policeman in the family. There are so many criminals about these days that one can't be too careful, don't you think?'

His mouth twitched in amusement.

'You appear to be developing a most unbecoming sense of humour, Mrs. Marchmont,' he said.

'Do I? It must be the weather,' said Angela.

She moved further away from him and placed herself deliberately so that there was a table between them. She was quite determined not to make a fool of herself over him again as she had in Italy, and flattered herself that she was doing well so far. Of course, he was perfectly aware that he was safe from her—that she would never give him away to the police, but that was as far as it went.

'So then, to what do I owe the pleasure of this visit?' she went on with great formality.

'Oh, nothing in particular,' he said. 'I just happened to be passing and thought I'd drop in.'

'Have you been in Italy all this time?' she said.

'Not all the time, no,' he said. 'I tend to move around, rather. I spent most of the summer there, though, recovering from an injury. You might remember it.'

'Of course I do,' said Angela, softening a little. 'Are you all right now?'

'Quite all right, thank you. Just the occasional twinge whenever a woman points a gun at me.'

That made her laugh.

'I don't suppose that happens *very* often, even to you,' she said.

'Not too often, no,' he said.

They smiled at one another for a moment, then he began, 'As a matter of fact, there *was* something—' but got no further before the doorbell rang loudly.

'Whoever can that be?' said Angela, as Marthe emerged and squinted through the peep-hole. 'Someone must have let them in downstairs.'

'It is M. Pilkington-Soames,' said Marthe, with a glance at Valencourt.

'Freddy! Don't let him in!' said Angela in a sudden panic, but it was too late, for the ring was followed by a knock and a muffled voice, which called:

'Don't bother trying to pretend you're not at home, Angela—I can hear you. Open the door. My mother won't let me back in the house until you've bought all her raffle tickets.'

'Quick! You'll have to hide,' said Angela. 'If he finds you here I'll never hear the last of it. He's a reporter, and a very inquisitive one at that,' she said in answer to his questioning look.

'How remarkably inconvenient,' said Valencourt, as she chivvied him towards the nearest door, which happened to lead to her bedroom.

'Don't come out until I tell you,' she said.

'You seem rather—er—practised at this,' he said. 'Do you do it often?'

'Not more than once or twice a day. You'll find the others hiding in the wardrobe,' she said as she shut the door on him. She had no time to wonder what had possessed her to make such an idiotic remark before Marthe opened the door to admit Freddy Pilkington-Soames, who rolled in looking dishevelled and as though he had been up all night. He looked around suspiciously as he entered.

'What was all that noise I heard just now?' he said. 'I thought there was someone here.'

'No,' said Angela, busying herself with the lilies as Marthe spotted Valencourt's hat and whisked it away behind Freddy's back. 'There's only me. And Marthe, of course. What was that you said about raffle tickets? Why didn't Cynthia come herself?'

'She said you'd be more likely to buy them from me,' said Freddy. 'Her exact words were, "You do it, darling—you know how susceptible she is to handsome young men."'

'Is that so?' said Angela, narrowing her eyes.

'I know, she has the most awful cheek,' said Freddy. 'She's right, though. How could you possibly refuse such a vision of angelic beauty and innocence?'

'That's not *quite* how I'd describe you,' said Angela, 'but of course I won't refuse. How much to make her stop bothering me, do you think?'

'Ten bob ought to do it, I reckon.'

'Here,' said Angela, digging in her handbag and handing him a crumpled note. 'What's the prize? Not another pig, I hope.'

'I've no idea. The usual, I expect. You'll have to ask her. I say, what's the hurry?' he said, for she was showing signs of wanting to usher him out. 'I was going to ask you to come out to tea with me.'

'Not now, Freddy,' she said. 'Marthe's going away and I have things to do. As a matter of fact I was just about to have a bath.'

'But if Marthe's going away you'll need someone to help you,' he said. 'I can hold the towel if you like.'

'Out!' she said, and pushed him towards the door. He was finally persuaded to leave, and she returned to the sitting-room, half-laughing, hoping that Valencourt had not overheard too much of the exchange.

'You can come out now,' she said, opening the bedroom door.

'He sounds like an interesting young man,' remarked Valencourt as he emerged.

'Oh, Freddy's quite incorrigible,' said Angela. 'I like him very much.'

At that moment Marthe appeared, wearing her coat and hat and carrying a little suitcase.

'If that is all, *madame*, then I will go,' she announced.

'Yes, thank you Marthe,' said Angela. 'Do give your mother my best wishes. Oh, and you'd better leave your key in case I need it.'

'Very well, I will leave it here,' said Marthe, putting the article in question on a little table. Then she bade them goodbye and left. Now they were quite alone, and Angela felt all the awkwardness return. There was a silence. She knew she ought to invite him to sit down, but feared it might encourage him to stay. He made no move, however, but merely stood there, looking at her.

'I seem to have caught you at a busy moment,' he said at last.

'Not at all. As a matter of fact this week has been very quiet up to now,' she said.

'Still, perhaps I oughtn't to have turned up like this. I'm a tremendous nuisance to you, I know, but I'm afraid I couldn't help myself.'

Angela opened her mouth to contradict him, but could not say the words, because of course he *was* a tremendous nuisance—there was no denying it.

'You were going to say something,' she said instead.

'Yes,' he replied. He hesitated, then went on, 'I don't suppose it'll be of much interest to you, given your earlier stated opinions on the subject of my character, but I wanted to let you know that I've decided to retire.'

Whatever Angela had expected, it was not this. She glanced up, and was surprised to find that he looked almost embarrassed.

'Oh,' she said. She was about to go on when there was a loud knock at the door, followed by a series of rings at the bell, which made her jump.

'I thought you said you weren't busy,' said Valencourt.

'It's Marthe again. She must have forgotten something,' said Angela. 'She needn't have made such a racket, though.'

She went into the little entrance-hall and opened the door, expecting her maid to hurry in apologetically. Instead, she was confronted by a most unexpected and unwelcome sight. Her heart gave a great thump, and she stared in shock and dismay at the man who stood before her, smiling from ear to ear.

'Hallo, Angie,' said the newcomer.

'Davie!' said Angela when she found her voice. 'What on earth are you doing here?'

'Why, I came to see you, of course,' he said. 'You might look more pleased to see me.' Then, as she made no move, he said, 'Well, don't just stand there. Aren't you going to invite me in?'

He did not wait for her to reply but instead pushed past her and into the house. Angela's head was in a whirl, but she exerted herself to be calm and act as though everything were quite normal.

'I guess you're doing well for yourself,' he said, looking around him as he entered the sitting-room. He caught sight of Valencourt and stiffened. 'Oh, I'm sorry,' he said. 'I didn't realize you had a visitor. I guess that'll teach me not to call first.'

He grinned genially and held out a hand. Valencourt took it with some reserve.

There was no getting around it now. Angela pulled herself together with the utmost effort.

'This is Mr. Smart, Davie,' she said, at her most distant and imperious. 'Mr. Smart, this is David Marchmont, my husband.'

CHAPTER TWO

I T WAS ALL terribly awkward, of course. Fortunately, Valencourt had sized up the situation immediately and was at his blandest and most self-effacing. Davie Marchmont, meanwhile, helped himself to an apple from a nearby bowl of fruit, threw himself into a chair and smiled broadly as though it had never occurred to him to doubt his welcome. To judge by the strong smell of spirits that hung about him, he was in drink.

'So you're a friend of Angie's, I guess,' he said.

'Yes,' said Valencourt. 'Or rather, my mother is.'

'Do thank her kindly for me,' said Angela, jumping on this with relief, and inwardly blessing the fact that Valencourt was still wearing his coat. 'Of course I'll come on Sunday. I wouldn't miss it for the world.'

'She'll be very pleased to hear it,' said Valencourt.

Angela escorted him to the front door and handed him his hat. He glanced warily towards the sitting-room and turned a questioning gaze on her, but she gave a little shake of her head.

'I'll see you all on Sunday, then,' she said brightly.

'Don't forget to bring your raffle tickets,' he said, and then he was gone, leaving Angela alone with her husband—the last person she wanted to see at that moment.

She returned to the sitting-room, where Davie had now wandered across to the window and was idly pulling open the drawers in a little chest and glancing into them as though he were quite in his own home. He was a tall, well-built man who had obviously once been handsome, but too much alcohol and too many late nights had done little for his appearance, and he was now running distinctly to seed. His skin wore an unattractive sheen and there was a thickening around the jaw and the waist that spoke of an excess of self-indulgence over the years, but despite this, he was still an imposing presence.

'Congratulations,' he said without turning round, as she entered the room. 'I liked your little pantomime just then. You don't think it fooled me for a second, do you?'

'What are you doing here, Davie?' said Angela. 'I thought you were in New York.'

'You mean you *hoped* I was in New York, to judge by what I just saw,' he said. He turned away from the window. 'Who is he? I guess he's not too fussy about whether a woman's married or not.'

'Don't be absurd, Davie,' said Angela. 'He's an acquaintance of mine. You don't suppose I sit at home all day, avoiding people, do you? I have lots of friends—both women and men—and they're all quite welcome to visit if they like. But never mind all that. Why are you here? I thought I'd made it quite clear before I left the States that I wanted nothing more to do with you.'

'That may be so,' he said, still wearing that self-satisfied smile of his, 'but I never said I wanted nothing more to do with *you*. And who knew whether you were serious or not? Married couples fight all the time, but they make it up again often enough. If you really meant it, then why didn't you divorce me when you had the chance?'

'That was a mistake on my part,' said Angela. 'I ought to have done it before I came here.'

'Well, you didn't, and from what I hear it's a little more difficult in this country to get rid of a husband you don't want. That's good news for me, I guess.'

'What do you mean?' said Angela, taken aback.

'Why, it means that you still belong to me, and that's how it ought to be, don't you agree?'

'Don't be ridiculous. You wanted the separation as much as I did,' said Angela.

'Is that what you think?' he said. 'Then you're wrong. You're my wife. Why would I want to let you go?'

He took a step forward and tried to put his arms around her, but she shook him off and stepped away.

'Is that any way to treat me?' he said, quite unabashed. 'Don't tell me you don't love me any more.'

'Of course I don't love you any more,' said Angela. 'Sometimes I wonder whether I ever did. Listen, Davie, I presume this is all a joke on your part, but I can assure you I don't find it very funny. We agreed to separate a long time ago, and I expected you to keep to your side of the bargain. Oh, *I* see,' she said, as a sudden realization struck her. 'You want money, don't you? You've spent what I gave you and now you want more. That's it, isn't it?' She gave a short laugh. 'Still the same old Davie, I see. You won't lift a finger for yourself but you're quite happy to live off your wife.'

'What if I am? I'm not fit to work, you know that. What choice do I have?'

'Not fit to work, indeed,' she said scornfully. 'Only because you think it's beneath you. You weren't too proud to let me support you, though.'

'And you never missed an opportunity to rub it in, did you? Making me come and beg for money, keeping me short. A wife ought not to embarrass her husband, but that's what you did. I could never make a show.'

'In front of all the other women, you mean? I see. It wasn't enough for you to humiliate me with your unfaithfulness—you wanted me to fund it too, is that it? Well, I told you when I left that I wouldn't give you another penny, and I meant it. You've come a long way for nothing, I'm afraid.'

They glared at one another furiously, Angela trembling slightly as years of resentment that she had thought long smoothed over rose to the surface. How she had hated all the rows and the recriminations! It had been nothing but misery almost from the start, and now, just as she was congratulating herself on having escaped and created a happy, contented life for herself in England, here he was again, bringing up the past and all the old feelings she had worked so hard to bury. Was there no end to it?

Davie regarded his wife calculatingly and changed tack.

'Listen, Angie,' he said wheedlingly. 'I didn't mean to get you all riled up. I just thought that after all this time you and I might be able to talk to one another without fighting.'

'There's nothing to talk about,' said Angela coldly. 'I haven't changed my mind. As soon as I am able, I shall file for a divorce, and until then I should be very glad if you would leave me alone.'

'I told you, you can't divorce me,' he said. 'Not here, anyway. You have no grounds. You ought to have done it back in the States while you had the chance. Here you'd have to prove adultery on my part, and you won't do that—just you try! I'm smart enough to be careful.'

Angela's heart sank. Of course he was right.

'As a matter of fact,' he went on meaningfully, 'I wonder what would happen if I did a little digging into *your* life here. You're a good-looking woman, Angie, and you're still young enough to want to have fun. I'll bet you get plenty of attention. What exactly have you been getting up to in the last couple of years? I saw the look that passed between you and that fellow just now. A friend of his mother, are you? How long do you think it would take a private detective to find out whether that's true or not? How would you like to have it all brought out in court and hear yourself called an adulteress? That would look good in the newspapers, don't you think?'

While he spoke he had advanced slowly upon her, and for a few seconds she stood frozen in fear. Then the spell broke, and she regarded him with disdain.

'Do as you please,' she said. 'But you may as well save your money, because you won't find anything.'

'Are you quite sure of that?' he said. 'Don't forget, I know all about you. You weren't exactly all white when I married you, were you? How would you like everyone to know about that?'

Again she felt the thrill of fear, but hid it.

'It's a pity you never wanted to give me children,' he went on. 'Maybe that's where things started to go wrong between us. It's not right to deny a man an heir. Kind of unnatural on the part of a woman, don't you think?'

Angela said nothing, and he again gave that self-satisfied smile.

'Still, never say die, eh?' he said. 'I don't have to worry about that any more. Not now. Not all women are as frozen as you.'

'How much do you want?' she said suddenly, and his smile widened.

'Well, now,' he said. 'I thought that might bring you round.'

'You haven't brought me round at all. I want you to leave, and I want to know how much it will cost me to get rid of you.'

His smile was so wide now that he was practically grinning from ear to ear. He came slowly towards her. Angela smelt the alcohol on him again and felt slightly sick.

'Suppose you suggest a figure,' he said.

CHAPTER THREE

F OR THE NEXT day or two Angela existed in a state of permanent nervousness and agitation. Davie's visit had upset her greatly, but she had hoped that once she gave him some money he would leave her alone—or, better still, go straight back to America. To her dismay, however, he turned up again on Thursday and announced that he would be more than happy to give her a divorce as long as she signed an agreement to pay him a generous annual allowance for life. This she refused absolutely to do. He laughed, for he had not really expected her to accede to it, and said in that case perhaps he ought to come and live with her at the Mount Street flat for the time being, so as to make the money she had already given him last a little longer. There had been an unpleasant scene, but Angela got rid of him at last, and it was not until Friday that she noticed to her consternation that Marthe's key, which she had left on the table as she departed, was no longer there. Angela called a locksmith as soon as she discovered the loss, and asked him to come and change the lock, but he was unable to come before Monday, and so she knew she would spend the weekend worrying that Davie might turn up and let himself in whenever he felt like it. He had refused to say how long he was planning to stay in London, but it was perfectly obvious that he meant to make a deliberate nuisance of himself while he was here, and she feared that now she had given him money he would keep on coming back for more and never leave her alone.

All this agitation was not helped by Angela's worry that Edgar Valencourt might appear again and confirm Davie's suspicions about them. She had heard nothing from Valencourt since Wednesday, and wondered whether he had gone back to Italy or wherever it was he lived at present. If that were so, it was probably for the best, although it was a pity they had not had the chance to finish their conversation before Davie had turned up. Had he really meant it when he said he was retiring? There had been reports in the newspaper in the past day or two about a daring robbery in which some valuable jewellery had been stolen from a private collection at a house in Kent. A servant had been knocked out and the thief or thieves had made off through a broken window. Angela's heart had given a great thump when she read the story, but it did not sound like his way of doing things, and sure enough it soon emerged that the police believed the theft to be the work of a well-known and ruthless gang. Angela was relieved despite herself, for although she had always maintained carelessly that it was all the same to her whether Valencourt retired or not, since she would accept no responsibility for his moral character, that part of her which would forever have a weakness for him had always secretly hoped that he would give the thing up one day. Of course they had no future together, for even if he did decide to stop doing it, there was still the unavoidable fact that he was wanted by the police in several countries and would be in danger of arrest for the rest of his life. Nonetheless, she would have liked to hear more about what he intended to do with himself now.

By Saturday Angela had quite given up any hopes of seeing Valencourt again, so she was surprised when she returned from lunch with a friend to see a familiar figure standing in Mount Street, fifty yards or so away from her flat, apparently engaged in examining the window display of a picture-framing shop. She reached a decision and, glancing about, headed in his direction. She did not stop or turn her head when she reached him, but instead said as she passed:

'I'm going to the Park. You can follow me in five minutes if you like.'

It was a grey day, but dry at least. Angela found a bench not far from the Serpentine, from where there would be a good view of anybody approaching, and sat down. Sure enough, in a few minutes he joined her and sat down at the other end of the bench. Angela glanced about again.

'I thought you'd gone,' she said.

'You can't get rid of me that easily,' he replied. 'I'm sorry about the other day.'

'You weren't to know. Nor was I, for that matter.'

'Weren't you expecting him, then?'

'Goodness, no,' she said. 'I last saw him more than two years ago when I left New York. Rather stupidly, I thought he wouldn't follow me over here. It seems I was wrong.'

'You're not divorced, then?'

She gave a rueful sigh.

'Unfortunately not. I meant to do it—certainly ought to have done it, but somehow I never quite got around to it, and then I came back to England and he was a thousand miles away and so I thought it didn't matter. The separation was agreed and I considered myself free. But don't let's talk about him—he's not in the slightest bit important.'

'Then why are you so nervous?' said Valencourt.

'Nervous? I'm not nervous.'

'Yes you are. You're all tense and worried-looking, and you keep glancing about as though you're expecting someone to turn up.'

'Do I?' said Angela.

'Yes. If I didn't know better I'd say you were afraid.'

'Nonsense. If I were afraid then I shouldn't be here with you now,' she said without thinking, then could have kicked herself.

'Why?' he said, suddenly alert.

'Never mind. It doesn't matter.'

'Of course it does. He said something, didn't he? About us, I mean.'

She did not reply directly, but instead said, 'It was all empty threats, of course. It's not as though there's anything to find out.'

'Isn't there?' he said softly, and she looked up and was caught by a sudden jolt of remembrance.

'Not here—not in England,' she said, although she was aware as she spoke of how feeble that sounded.

'I suppose not,' he said. He paused for a moment, then went on, 'I didn't come here to make things difficult for you, Angela. As a matter of fact, I came to say goodbye.'

'Oh?' said Angela. 'Are you going away again?'

'Yes, and for good this time. I dare say that will be something of a relief to you.'

'But why? You said something about retiring—unless I misheard you. Is it to do with that?'

'No, you didn't mishear. I have decided to retire.'

'But why?' she said again.

'I don't know,' he said. 'After I was shot I had a little time to think while I was recovering, and I started to realize that it's not fun any more—I'm not quite sure why. Perhaps it's just that I'm getting too old for all this sort of nonsense.'

'*Was* it fun, once?'

'Oh, terribly good fun to start with. You can't imagine what a kick I got out of it. But I was a young man then, and I'd taken a few knocks that hurt me rather, and I felt the world owed me something. Very arrogant of me, I know, but there's youth for you. I was dreadfully complacent and full of myself for a very long time. I'm starting to tire of it all now, though. I can't go on doing it until I'm an old man. Sooner or later I won't have the energy to run any more.' He paused, then went on ruefully. 'And much as I hate to admit it, I appear to be developing a rudimentary conscience in my old age.'

'Dear me, how unfortunate for you,' said Angela. 'Where did that spring from?'

'I rather think it all started last May,' he said. 'There's a woman, you see,'

'Is there?' said Angela, raising her eyes to his.

'Yes,' he said, holding her gaze. 'It's all her fault. I met her in Italy and we got along rather well. She's a much better person than I am, but she refuses to take on the job of reforming me.'

'Does she? I'm not surprised. I don't think it's possible to reform someone. I think they have to reform themselves.'

'That's what she said, and I dare say she's right. Still, she is acting as my temporary conscience at present—just until mine grows strong enough to shift for itself.'

She laughed.

'Do you think it will?' she said.

'Who knows?' he said.

They smiled, then she said quietly:

'I'm glad.'

'Thank you. I hoped you would be. Of course, that doesn't alter the fact that I have done some rather dubious things in the past. It's not as though I can just come out into the open and settle down in the country with a wife and children. I'm willing to experiment with honesty but I draw the line at giving myself up.'

'Then what shall you do?' said Angela. Now she noticed for the first time that he seemed on edge too. He did not glance about as frequently as she did, but there was a nervousness about him that she had never seen before.

'I must leave,' he said. 'One unfortunate effect of this sort of life is that one mixes with people who have a tendency to

CLARA BENSON

resolve any little difficulty that may arise with violence. You saw it yourself in Italy. I'm afraid there's a good chance that I may have—er—offended someone, so I think the best thing will be for me to make myself scarce.'

'You're in danger?'

'It's entirely possible,' he admitted.

'Then where will you go?'

'I shall lie low for a month or two in France until the commotion dies down, then I shall go somewhere far away—perhaps South America. I believe they breed horses there. That's what I always meant to do, before—other things intervened.'

'South America? That's a long way,' said Angela.

'It is, but I expect it's pleasant enough. Naturally, I shall miss the old country, but it's not as though I spend much time here these days anyway.'

'I suppose not,' said Angela. The remark brought Davie back into her mind and she glanced around again.

'You're still nervous,' he said.

She shook herself.

'I oughtn't to be,' she said. 'Davie mentioned hiring a private detective, but of course they're very expensive and he hasn't that sort of money.'

'Don't worry,' said Valencourt. 'I've had plenty of experience of avoiding people, as you may imagine. There's no-one here you need concern yourself about.'

'I hate all this,' said Angela suddenly. 'I mean, all this skulking about in parks as though I had something to feel guilty about.'

'You have nothing to feel guilty about,' he said. 'We're having a perfectly innocent conversation.'

'That's debatable,' she said. 'I shouldn't like anybody to over-hear us.'

'There's nobody *to* overhear,' he said. 'Please don't worry. I must say, though, this husband of yours sounds like rather an ass.'

'He's a tremendous ass,' said Angela with some energy.

'It's a pity that being an ass isn't grounds for divorce.'

She gave a small smile.

'I believe it is, in the States,' she said. 'Although I don't think the law puts it in quite those terms.'

They fell silent for a few moments, watching people as they passed to and fro through the Park.

'I'm leaving in the morning,' he said at last. 'Will you come out with me tonight, Angela?'

'I can't,' said Angela contritely. 'I have to go to a charity ball. It's been organized by some friends of mine and I agreed to go ages ago. They'll never forgive me if I don't turn up.'

'That's a pity,' he said.

'But you could come. They'll be selling tickets at the door. You'll have no trouble getting in, I'm certain of it.'

'Should you like me to?'

'Yes, very much,' she said.

'Will your husband be there? I don't want to get you into trouble,' he said.

'No,' she said. 'He doesn't know any of my friends and there's no reason he should be there. It's not his sort of thing, anyway.'

'Isn't he staying at the flat with you?'

'No, of course not,' said Angela. 'He said something about staying at some club or other—Burkett's, I think—with an old friend of his.'

'Can I ask you to dance without anyone getting suspicious, do you suppose?'

'I dare say. It's easy enough to be inconspicuous in a crowd. One frequently ends up dancing with people one doesn't know.'

'Then I'll come, and we can say goodbye tonight,' he said.

She looked at her watch.

'I'd better go,' she said, and made to rise from the seat, but he had spotted something.

'What's that on your arm?' he said.

She rearranged her sleeve hurriedly.

'Nothing,' she said.

Before she could stop him he took hold of her hand and pushed back her coat sleeve to reveal a row of ugly bruises, black and purple, on her forearm. He looked questioningly at her but she would not meet his eye.

'Did he do this to you?' he said.

She pushed the sleeve down again and set her jaw, but said nothing.

'He did, didn't he?'

'He doesn't know his own strength,' she said carelessly. 'And I've always bruised easily.'

They both knew she was lying. His face darkened and a look of anger passed across it.

'Oh, Angela, I'm so terribly sorry,' was all he said.

'Don't be,' she said. 'He won't be here long. He'll get tired of plaguing me and go back to America, and then I'll divorce him and be rid of him at last.'

'But what if he doesn't?'

'Then I'll have to think of some other way of getting rid of him,' she said.

'Yes, but—'

'Enough,' she said. 'Listen, we've agreed he's an ass so let's leave it at that. I don't want to talk about him any more—as a matter of fact we've wasted far too much time in talking about him already. Now, I really must go as I have a lot to do. You will come this evening, won't you?'

'Try and stop me.'

'Splendid,' she said, and smiled suddenly. 'Then I'll see you tonight.'

And with that, she stood up and walked off briskly, leaving him sitting on the bench, gazing after her.

CHAPTER FOUR

THE WHITE RABBIT Ball was a charity event that had
been running for three or four years now, and was rapidly
becoming a fixture on the social calendar of a certain section
of London society. It had begun as a joke, after a promising
young artist had spent six months producing an experimental
sculpture of a gigantic white rabbit in papier mâché, which had
proceeded to collapse under the weight of its own over-sized
ears on the opening night of its first exhibition to the public.
Fortunately, the artist in question had seen the funny side, and
some bright soul had had the idea of turning it into a regular
thing with music and dancing and a light supper. Each year at
this time, therefore, the Duke of Wymington gave up his house
and his ball-room at the behest of his wife, who was a great
patron of the arts, and sat in his library, shuddering quietly, as
hundreds of people flocked through his front door, shrieking,
laughing, chipping the paint and ruining the carpets. Mean-

while, a white papier mâché rabbit, produced on the model of the original but filled with balloons, was placed as the grand decoration of honour at one end of the ball-room. At midnight a bell would sound, giving the signal for all the revellers (by now usually very drunk) to attack the rabbit with anything that came to hand—forks, knives, shoes and many other things besides—until it lay in smithereens and all the balloons were set free.

This year's ball looked like being every bit as riotous as its predecessors, and when Angela arrived in company with the Pilkington-Soameses and some other friends she found the place already hot, crowded and deafening. On the one hand this boded well, for it meant that nobody was likely to notice if she spent part of the evening in company with Edgar Valencourt, but on the other there was some doubt as to whether they would be able to find one another at all in the throng.

'Come and dance,' said Freddy once they had found their table and sat down. 'It's bad enough now, but it'll be unbearable after supper once people have started being sick on the floor.'

Ignoring Angela's pained expression, he took her hand and pulled her into the middle of the heaving crowd.

'So, then, what have you been getting up to lately?' he said. 'You hurried me out of the house so quickly the other day that we didn't have time to chat. What have you been doing with yourself?'

'Not much,' she replied. 'Very little, in fact. It's been a very quiet week. Marthe has left me and all my friends keep falling ill or dropping dead when I want to go and see them.'

'Inconsiderate of them.'

'Well, quite. I think this is the first time I've been out in about a fortnight.'

'You ought to have called me,' said Freddy. 'We might have gone out together. As a matter of fact there was rather a good night at the Express Club about ten days ago. All the old crowd were there—all the fun people: Bill Arnott, Mags Bagley—Gertie, of course. You ought to have come.'

'I think they're all a little young for me,' said Angela. 'I'm not twenty-one any more, much as I weep to admit it.'

'I refuse to believe it,' said Freddy stoutly. 'You are as young and lively as you ever were.'

'Thank you, Freddy,' said Angela. 'You're terribly kind and I choose to believe you. But what about you? How is business at the *Clarion*? Have they promoted you to editor yet?'

'Incredible as it may seem, they have not,' said Freddy. 'Anyway, I don't know that I want to be editor any more. I rather enjoy getting out and about.'

'Are you pursuing any exciting stories at the moment?'

'Well, of course the big one at the moment is this jewel robbery in Kent,' he said.

A frown flickered across Angela's forehead.

'It's a gang, isn't it?' she said.

'Yes, the Boehler gang. They're a bunch of ruffians and the sooner they're caught the better.'

Angela could not help asking half-fearfully:

'Are the police quite sure it's them? They don't suspect anyone else?'

'Oh, no, it was certainly them,' said Freddy. 'They're quite brazen and don't bother to wear gloves, so the police have their finger-prints.'

'Are they foreigners? That doesn't sound like an English name.'

'Yes, they're German, I think,' said Freddy. 'Or possibly Austrian. They've been marauding about the capital cities of Europe for some time now, leaving a trail of violence and broken glass in their wake. It's all terribly vulgar.'

Angela's brow cleared.

'Goodness,' she said. 'They sound quite dreadful. Still, at least you ought to have plenty to write about for a while.'

The dance finished and they returned to their table to find the waiter just arriving with drinks. Angela was becoming increasingly nervous at the prospect of seeing Edgar Valencourt and found herself drinking a little more than she had intended, but quickly realized what she was doing and stopped. It would not do to be muddle-headed when they met—if indeed he turned up, for she had seen no sign of him so far. Perhaps he had changed his mind or been unable to get in. The thought dismayed her more than she cared to admit, and she spent the first part of the evening in a state of some preoccupation.

It was not until after supper that she spotted him, standing by the edge of the dance floor, not looking at her. She was passing with a little group of ladies, and deliberately allowed the others to get ahead of her. Valencourt watched until they had disappeared out of sight, then turned to her.

'Awful crowd here,' he said.

'Terrible, isn't it?' she said. 'It's like this every year. I don't know why I agreed to come.'

'You look quite beautiful,' he said.

'Thank you,' she said, glancing down at her dress, which was not the one she had originally intended to wear, for she had had to substitute her first preference for a frock that went with long gloves.

'Will you dance with me?' he said.

She gave him her widest smile. She could not help it.

'I should be delighted,' she said.

He led her on to the floor and very soon they were pressed as close together as public decency would allow.

'What shall you say if your friends ask who I am?' he said.

'Oh, I shall just say that I know you slightly from some committee or other, and that you're very worthy and polite but rather dull,' she said. 'Just to allay suspicion, of course.'

'Of course,' he said.

She adopted the most convincing bored look she could muster.

'What do you think?' she said. 'Do I look as though I'm finding your company too terribly tedious?'

'Oh, absolutely.'

'Then nobody will ever suspect a thing,' she said.

'You have the advantage of me, I'm afraid,' he said. 'I could never even pretend to find you dull.'

'You say the nicest things,' said Angela. 'It's a pity you have to leave. I could keep you in a box and bring you out to cheer me up whenever I was feeling particularly cross or out of sorts.'

'I'd do that and welcome,' he said. 'But I'd rather you didn't keep me in a box.'

'No. I expect you'd get rather creased after a while. Very well, I shall let you go wherever you choose, and find another way of cheering myself up whenever I need it.'

'I see one of your friends has spotted us,' he said, and she glanced back and saw Freddy standing not far off, looking at them.

'Freddy. I might have known,' she said, assuming her bored expression again.

'So that's Freddy, is it? The inquisitive reporter.'

'Yes. He hasn't been doing it long, but I think he'll get on very well, since he has morals of indiarubber.'

'Is that so?' said Valencourt, regarding the young man with interest.

Freddy was no longer looking at them, and shortly afterwards moved away. Angela and Valencourt turned their attention back to one another and resumed their conversation—which could hardly be called a conversation in the usual sense of the word, being rather an exchange of agreeable nonsense between two people who were far more pleased with each other than they had any right to be. Angela's head was spinning slightly, but whether that were because of the cocktails or the company she could not say; perhaps it was a little of both. She was thankful that this would be the last time she saw him, and perhaps for that reason was slightly less reserved than she might otherwise have been, for until then she had always attempted to maintain a certain degree of coolness in her manner towards him. She was aware that they might be under observation, however, and did her best not to give herself away *too* much, flattering herself that any outsider glancing casually at them for a second would never suppose them to be anything more than friends.

She had reckoned without Freddy, however. That young man had seen Angela Marchmont dancing with a man he did not know, and at first had thought nothing of it, for although the man was rather good-looking Angela appeared more bored than anything. Freddy sympathized silently with the suffering which a dull dancing partner could bring, wondered for half a second who the man was and then turned his attention elsewhere. A minute or so later, however, he happened to glance in their direction again and this time saw an entirely different picture, for now the man was murmuring something into Angela's ear in a most familiar way. She did not draw back but listened, then her face broke into a wide smile and she said something, shaking her head at him. The man said something else and Angela glanced around, caught sight of Freddy and turned suddenly serious again. Freddy raised his eyebrows and wandered deliberately out of their sight, but did not take his eyes off them. This time there was no mistaking what was going on, because just then, for the merest few seconds, a look and a smile passed between the two of them which immediately answered any questions in Freddy's mind as to their true connection with one another. They looked away again quickly, but for those few seconds nobody could have doubted the affinity between them.

Freddy pursed his lips in a silent whistle.

'Well, well,' he thought, and wondered again, this time with much more interest, who the man was. Angela was not a woman who liked to talk about her private concerns—indeed, until that moment Freddy had always imagined, without thinking too deeply about it, that she had none, for she had always seemed to prefer to mix with a wide circle of close acquaintances rather than any one person in particular. Where Mr. Marchmont was Freddy did not know, but he had always assumed somehow that there had been a divorce in America and that that was why Angela had returned to England. She was rarely seen out in company with any male companion; nor did this seem to bother her, and so Freddy had fallen into the idle assumption that she was happiest on her own—although he now remembered having been briefly suspicious last summer that there had been some entanglement. She had admitted nothing, however, and so he had believed he must have been mistaken. But of course, now he came to think about it, it was highly unlikely that there should be no-one on the scene, and it was rapidly dawning on him as he stood there that in fact Angela was not so much fiercely independent of any man as merely very discreet.

A malicious grin spread across Freddy's face as he resolved to make the very most of this new knowledge. Of course, he was very fond of Angela, but to miss such an opportunity to tease her unmercifully whenever the opportunity presented itself would be to betray all his most dearly-held principles. Besides, she was quite capable of giving as good as she got, and so there was no need at all for him to tread lightly. He would call on her tomorrow, he decided—not too early, of course—and begin his campaign of torment, although tonight he would content himself with merely dropping one or two hints. He wondered whether she would introduce the man to their party. It would be interesting to talk to him and find out what exactly it took to attract Angela, who did not normally appear to be easily impressed by the opposite sex.

He was reflecting pleasurably on the prospect of getting a rise out of his friend when he was accosted by a young lady of his acquaintance, who declared it was an age since they had seen one another and insisted that he come and meet her new fiancé. Freddy allowed her to lead him away and put his new knowledge to the back of his mind, resolving to save it for later. He was quite determined that Angela should not escape him, but it would have to wait for now.

CHAPTER FIVE

AFTER THE DANCE finished Angela and Valencourt made their way out of the ballroom in search of some fresh air and quiet. Unfortunately, the corridor outside was full of people who had had the same idea—mainly giggling couples and men looking for a brief respite from their arduous social duties—and in the end they were forced to stand almost by the front door of the house and put up with the occasional blast of cold air whenever someone went in or out. Angela stood by a tall potted palm and did her best not to glance around nervously.

'What time do you leave tomorrow?' she said.

'Early,' he replied. 'The boat train departs at half past seven. I should be in Calais by early afternoon, I think.'

'Then you really are going to France,' she said.

'Of course,' he said. 'Where did you think I was going?'

'I don't know,' she said. 'It might be anywhere. I'm afraid I still never quite know whether you're telling the truth or not.'

'But why should I lie in this instance?'

'No reason at all. You must have realized by this time that I'm unlikely to set the police on you,' she said dryly.

He smiled.

'I don't take you for granted, I assure you,' he said. 'Quite the contrary, in fact. If *you* never know whether or not I'm telling the truth, *I* never know whether or not you'll give me the cold shoulder when we meet.'

'Then it appears we're even,' she said, and accepted a cigarette from him.

He put his hand in his inside pocket for a light and accidentally half-pulled something out with it. He replaced it immediately, but it was too late, for although the corridor was only dimly lit, they were standing directly below a ceiling lamp, which gleamed off whatever it was and threw it into sharp relief for the merest second. Angela saw it immediately and stiffened.

'What was that?' she said.

Was it her imagination, or did a guilty look flash briefly across his face?

'What was what?' he said.

'That thing you pulled out of your pocket just now.'

'This, you mean?' he said, bringing out a cigarette-lighter. 'It's empty. Rather pointless carrying it around, really.'

Had they not just been talking about his trustworthiness or otherwise, Angela might have let it go at that, but despite what she had said only a moment ago, this time she knew for certain that he was lying. She looked into his face and forced him to meet her gaze.

'No, that's not what I meant and you know it,' she said. 'What was it? Something you oughtn't to have?'

'Of course not,' he said, and all the lightness had suddenly gone from his tone.

They regarded one another warily, adversaries once again. There was a pause, then Angela lifted her chin.

'Goodbye, Mr. Valencourt,' she said coldly, and with that turned on her heel and walked back towards the ball-room. She was furious with him and with herself. She had thought that they might part on good terms at least, but here he was, lying to her once again. He had talked of giving up his life of crime, and yet she had seen as plainly as anything what he had been carrying in his pocket. How stupid she had been to believe him! He had evidently not changed one bit—would never change, in fact—and it was high time she forgot about the man once and for all, for he would bring nothing but disappointment.

'Wait!' he said, and followed her up the corridor. They stopped by the door to the ballroom and Angela regarded him inquiringly, doing her best to hide her anger under a calm exterior.

'What is it?' she said.

'Don't go. Will you let me explain?' he said.

In any other circumstances she would have said no, for listening to him would only serve to give him yet another opportunity to do what he did so well: try and win her over with words. Now, however, she saw a look on his face she had never seen before—a look of genuine concern, perhaps even anxiety, at what had just happened, and it disconcerted her, for she had never known him to appear anything other than perfectly pleased with himself. But what could he possibly have to say in justification? As far as they could they had always avoided talking about his crimes, the thing that would forever stand between them. Angela did not want to know anything, for the subject pained her, and he had had the sense and the good manners to refrain from making an accessory of her by pressing the knowledge on to her. But now it looked as though they would have to have it out once and for all—here, in the most public of places. Angela felt the anger rise again at the idea of being forced into such a conversation at such a time, but after a moment's thought she merely said, without the slightest hint of a smile:

'I shall give you five minutes, but not here. We'd better go somewhere private.'

She indicated another dimly-lit passage that led off at right angles to the one they were in, and set off along it without looking to see whether he were following. She had been on the organizing committee for the previous year's ball, and re-membered that down here was the room they had used as an office. She stopped halfway along the passage, opened a door and switched on a light to reveal a tiny box-room—little more than a large cupboard, in fact, which contained nothing but a desk and chair, one or two small cabinets and a few untidy piles of paper. Valencourt shut the door behind them and turned to her. There was a silence as they regarded each other warily again, then after a long moment he put his hand reluctantly into his inside pocket and brought something out. It had been wrapped in a handkerchief but had partly escaped its makeshift covering, which was how Angela had spotted it.

'I ought to have rolled it up more tightly,' he said.

'Is that what you think?' she said.

He held the thing out to her and for an instant she recoiled, but then curiosity got the better of her and she slowly reached out and took it. It was a brooch, a little smaller than the palm of her hand, set with clusters of diamonds, and with one great ruby the size of her thumb-nail in the centre. The light glimmered off it, dazzling and mesmerizing her, and for one mad second she could almost understand why it was he did what he did. But then the spell broke, and she handed it back quickly and said:

'Did you steal it?'

'Not exactly,' he said.

'Either you did or you didn't,' she said.

He fell silent for a moment, and seemed to be debating with himself as to what to tell her. At last, he said:

'There was a robbery a few days ago at a house in Kent. You may have read something about it.'

'Yes,' she said, and her heart sank. 'I did, but I didn't think it sounded like your work.'

'It wasn't. An old man was hit on the head while it was going on. I don't like that sort of thing—never have. There was no need for violence.'

'But you have some connection to the thieves,' she said.

'Unfortunately, yes. I won't bore you with the whole story, but some time ago when it was all being planned I agreed to take some of the stuff off their hands and dispose of it. It's not something I'd normally do, but at the time I didn't have any choice, for reasons I won't go into, so I said I'd do it.'

'I see,' she said.

'The man I was dealing with said it would be an easy job, and that they'd be in and out within minutes. It's a private collection, you see. It's not like a museum where there'd be bars on the windows, guards, and suchlike. This chap said nobody would even find out they'd been in until the next morning. I didn't like or trust him, and didn't want to mix with his associates, who are a pretty notorious lot—yes, even among our circles—but I told myself it would be a matter of meeting the fellow after the job, taking the stuff and disappearing.

'Of course, as it turned out it wasn't as simple as that. First of all they whacked that old fellow on the head. I hadn't agreed to that —in fact, I'd made it quite clear that I wouldn't be associated with that sort of thing. Then they wanted me to shelter two of them for a week or so, just until the hue and cry died down, even though I'd said I hadn't the slightest intention of seeing any of them again after the job was done. And on top of all that they tried to back out on the price we'd originally agreed. By that point I could see quite well the way things were going, and I had no desire to get into an argument, so I—er—took something as payment for my time and made myself scarce.'

'And you think that's not stealing?' said Angela, aghast.

'Well, yes, I suppose it is,' he admitted. 'But I didn't plan it, exactly. It was a spur of the moment thing. Old habits die hard and I simply couldn't help myself.'

He gazed wistfully at the ruby brooch in his hand.

'But it's not *yours*,' said Angela.

'I know, but I'm afraid I couldn't resist it. It's so awfully pretty.' Before she could reply he approached her and held it up to her breast, where it sparkled against the black of her dress. 'Don't you think it would look beautiful on you?' he said in his most persuasive tones.

She pushed his hand away and took a step back.

'Don't!' she said. 'I don't want the thing near me, and if you think you can win me round with that sort of nonsense you're very wrong indeed. Oh, what's the use?' she went on, throwing up her hands. 'I can see there's no sense at all in trying to talk to you. I'd better go. My friends will be wondering where I am.'

'No!' he said quickly. 'Don't go. I'm sorry.'

'Sorry you took it? Or sorry I found you out?' said Angela. He did not reply, and she continued, 'Look, it's perfectly obvious this is something we'll never agree on. You think it's all just fun—a terribly good joke. But it's not; it's wrong, and however much you try to pass it off as something quite innocent, nothing changes the fact that it's theft—pure and simple.'

She paused, then before she could stop herself admitted the thing which had hurt the most.

'But why did you have to bring me into it, Edgar?' she said quietly. 'Why did you have to lie to me on top of everything? Silly of me, but I really believed you meant it when you said you were going to retire. You needn't have said that at all. I already knew what you were; I had no expectations of you. Then why make a fool of me again? Is it just because you can?'

'Please don't say that,' said Valencourt. 'I never dreamt of trying to make a fool of you. I promise you I was telling the truth. This was my last job and I won't be doing any more. It's just unfortunate that it turned out the way it did, since it means I'll have to disappear rather more quickly than I intended. But I swear I haven't lied to you. Not this time.'

'I take it these people are looking for you, then.'

'I'm afraid so,' he said. 'And not to shake my hand, either.'

'So that's why you're planning to lie low,' said Angela. 'I see now. And what do you intend to do with the brooch?'

'I shall find some way of getting rid of it,' he said. 'There's always a market for these things.'

'Give it back,' she said suddenly.

'What?'

'You heard me. Give it back. It's not yours.'

'But that won't help. They're not the forgiving sort.'

'I didn't mean that. I meant give it back to its rightful owners. They've lost their whole jewellery collection, so of course this won't put things right, but at least it will go some way to making amends.'

He gazed at her blankly.

'But—' he began.

'Is it so difficult to understand?' she said. 'I thought I'd made myself clear enough.'

'What do you suggest I do?' he said. 'Wrap it in brown paper and post it back to them with an apology?'

'If you like,' she said.

'Why, that's absurd,' he said. He seemed astonished at the whole idea.

'Listen,' she said, 'if you really meant what you said about giving it all up then you'll do it. But don't insult me by claiming that you're going to retire for my sake when all the time you're wandering around with stolen rubies in your pocket. I won't stand for it. If you're really serious about this, and if you really care in the slightest what I think of you—which I doubt—'

'Of course I care what you think of me.'

'Then do it,' she said.

Her expression held a challenge.

'All right,' he said after a moment's hesitation. 'I will.'

'When?'

'I don't know. Now, if you like.'

'Are you sure?' said Angela, caught off guard, since she had been quite certain that he would make his excuses and leave.

'Why not? I'm going away tomorrow, so the sooner the better.'

'But how?' said Angela. 'You're not really going to post it, are you?'

'It's not that far—not much more than an hour's drive at this time of night, I shouldn't think. I shall take it in person.'

Angela stared at him, astounded. She had not expected this at all.

'Good,' she managed weakly. 'I'm glad.'

'But how will you know I've done it, if you won't take my word?' he said.

She did not deny the implication, but came to a sudden decision. If he could be reckless, then so could she.

'I'll come with you,' she said. 'If you will insist on my acting as your conscience then I suppose I ought to rise to the occasion.'

His face broke into a smile.

'Splendid,' he said. 'Then let's go.'

CHAPTER SIX

THEY LEFT AT midnight, when the revellers were just attacking the giant white rabbit with yells and shrieks of glee. Angela found a woman from her party and said that she was going home, and that she would take a taxi so please not to worry about her, then ran off before any questions could be asked. Then she and Valencourt slipped out unobserved through a side door and hurried to his motor-car, which was parked not far away. Soon they were speeding along the Old Kent Road out of London. The roads were almost deserted at that time of night, and they sat mostly in silence. Angela was lost in her own thoughts, half-convinced that she was in the middle of the strangest dream, and that any moment she would wake up and find herself in her own bed—for surely she could not *really* be driving into deepest Kent with a notorious thief, on a mission to replace a stolen jewel, could she? And yet it had been her own idea. It was really none of her business whether he returned the thing or not, and it would have been much wiser altogether to feign unconcern as to what became of him, but she had the oddest feeling that tonight was important, and that what happened in the next few hours would somehow affect both of them for a long time to come. It was a strange impression, and one she could not shake off, but she supposed that *anyone* would feel the same way if they were placed in the situation in which she now found herself—which, after all, was a highly unusual one.

At last they saw a sign for Faversham and Valencourt turned off the Kent road.

'Do you know where it is?' said Angela.

'I think so,' he replied. 'Luckily for us, it's on the outskirts of the town so we oughtn't to draw too much attention to ourselves.'

It now occurred to Angela to wonder what would happen if they were caught. Valencourt would be arrested, of course, but what would happen to her? Was it a crime to be in possession of stolen goods even if one intended to return them? She did not know. And what would the police say if they found her in company with a known criminal? For the first time Angela was forced to consider whether or not she ought to deny all knowledge of his activities if she were ever questioned on the subject. Of course, it would be a cowardly thing to do, but equally there would be little sense in admitting to knowing who he was, for it was not as though she had ever stolen anything herself and she had always done her best to distance herself from him—with very little success, it was true, but her intentions were good. She was quite certain that Valencourt would advise her not to confess anything, but her conscience was uncomfortable.

After a few minutes' consideration, she decided very sensibly that it would be much better not to get caught at all, and put the thing out of her mind.

They drove along country roads for a mile or two, then Valencourt stopped the car.

'We'd better walk from here,' he said. 'A car will be too noisy at this time of night.'

'It's not far, is it?' said Angela, who was not dressed for muddy lanes.

'Only a quarter of a mile or so,' he said.

Fortunately, the road was not too dirty, and soon they saw a pair of tall gate-posts ahead of them. Through them, Angela could just see the outline of a large house a short distance away.

'Well, here goes,' said Valencourt, and fished in his pocket for the brooch.

'Hadn't you better wipe the finger-prints off it first?' said Angela.

'I don't suppose you'd take it as a compliment if I told you you'd make a good criminal?' he said.

'Not exactly,' she said.

He wiped the brooch and wrapped it carefully in the handkerchief, then, placing a finger over his lips, he took her hand and they tiptoed up the path together. The house was in pitch blackness and all was silent. Angela found herself holding her breath. She would not admit it, but she was afraid, fearing that lights would suddenly go on and dogs would start to bark, and it would be all up with them. But everything remained quiet and they reached the front door without incident.

They stood under the portico and Angela regarded Valencourt expectantly. He looked at the little bundle in his hand.

'Are you sure you don't want to keep it?' he said in a low voice.

'Quite sure.'

'Very well, then. Will you do it for me?'

'No, Edgar,' she said. 'I want to see you do it.'

'You're a hard woman,' he said. He hesitated for just a moment, then dropped it through the letter-box.

They returned to the car. Angela was fighting the urge to break into a run, but he walked at a leisurely pace as though they were strolling along the river on a Sunday afternoon.

'Back to London, then,' he said as he started the engine. 'Do you suppose your friends have noticed you've gone yet?'

'I told them I wasn't feeling well and that I'd get a taxi home,' she said. 'I ought to be quite safe.'

He glanced at her.

'Are you sure of that?' he said.

'What do you mean?'

'I don't like leaving you to the mercies of that fellow.'

'I told you, there's no need to worry about him. He's a nuisance, that's all. He wants money, and he'll probably hang around until I've given him enough to satisfy him for the present, then go away.'

'It's a pity you didn't divorce him when you had the chance,' he said.

'Yes,' she said. 'I didn't have time, though. I came away rather quickly in the end. I was frightened, you see. I thought something dreadful might happen if I didn't get away from him.'

He looked at her in surprise.

'You don't mean you were afraid he'd kill you?'

'No,' she said. 'Quite the opposite, in fact. I was afraid I'd kill him.'

He raised his eyebrows, but said nothing. They drove in silence for a few minutes, then suddenly Angela began to laugh.

'What is it?' he said.

'Nothing,' she said. 'Just that I shall never get over your ability to surprise me.'

He laughed too.

'As a matter of fact I've rather surprised myself this evening. I certainly never expected to be doing this. You wretched woman! Look what you've done to me. I shall never be able to hold my head up in public again.'

'I knew you couldn't be as black as you like to paint yourself,' she said.

'I suppose even the worst of us have our decent moments.'

'Were you good, once?' she said curiously.

'Perhaps not good,' he said. 'Can anyone be wholly good? I certainly wasn't as good as you, but I was better than I am now.'

'I'm not that good,' she said. 'I've done my share of bad things. I just don't boast about them.'

'Do I boast?'

'Just a little,' she said.

He laughed again.

'I suppose I do, now and again. I can't help but be pleased with myself. It's a weakness of mine. Am I insufferable?'

'Not *all* the time,' she said.

'Splendid,' he said. 'Then there's hope for me yet.'

'I suppose you're in some danger now,' she said after a pause. 'Do they know how to find you?'

'Not at this moment,' he said. 'Most criminals have the good sense to stay well away from the scene of the crime. They're hardly likely to be looking for me here.'

'But they will come looking?'

'Yes,' he said carelessly. 'They're rather a foul lot and they don't forget a bad turn in a hurry. I dare say they'll keep up the search for some time to come.'

'Aren't you afraid?' she said.

'One doesn't get far in this business by being afraid,' he said. 'I try and take these things lightly.'

'Can you protect yourself, though? Do you have a gun, or anything like that?'

'I don't like guns,' he said. 'They're noisy and fire things that hurt when they hit you.'

'All the more reason to have one yourself,' she said.

'Well, I don't own one, I'm afraid.'

'I have a gun,' she said after a moment. 'You can have it.'

'But I don't need it.'

'Perhaps not, but I'd like you to take it all the same.'

'If I didn't know better, I'd say you were concerned for my safety, Mrs. Marchmont,' he said.

'Let's pretend for the purposes of this conversation that I am,' she said.

'Yes, let's. I rather like the idea. It's a long time since anyone was concerned about me.'

'Then you'll take the gun?'

'Of course I will,' he said, 'since you insist on it.'

'I do,' she said.

They fell silent for a few moments, then he said:

'Am I to take it that I'm back in your good books now?'

They exchanged glances.

'Perhaps,' she replied.

'Then will you come and talk to me and keep me company while I pack my things? It's almost three o'clock and I shall be going in a few hours, and I'm afraid I left everything in rather a mess before I came out. Do say you will. You're not tired, are you?'

'No,' said Angela, who had never felt more awake. It had been the oddest of evenings, and she was still feeling strangely reckless and exhilarated after their midnight adventure. She knew she would find it impossible to sleep if she went home, so without giving it too much thought she agreed. After all, he would be gone for good soon, and she would never see him again—which would be a relief in many ways—so she saw no harm in granting his request and keeping him company for the few hours that remained to him in London. He seemed pleased, and the rest of the journey to London proceeded mostly in silence.

It was a quarter to seven and still dark when they arrived back at Angela's flat in Mount Street. Angela was nervous, for she feared that Davie might have taken it into his head to come to the flat and let himself in with Marthe's key, but her worries were swiftly dispelled when she turned on the light and found everything as she had left it. She peeped into one or two rooms but saw nobody.

'You can come in,' she said to Valencourt, who had been standing outside on the landing.

'Isn't Marthe back yet?' he said.

'No,' said Angela. 'I gave her a week. She'll be back on Wednesday.'

'Dear me. How will you manage?' he said mockingly.

'I'm not entirely incapable,' she said. 'I do know where things are kept, at least.' She went across to a chest of drawers by the window and opened the second drawer, then frowned and pulled open the top one instead. 'Ah, here it is,' she said, and handed him her little revolver. 'I keep it fully loaded.'

'Thank you,' he said, putting it in his pocket. 'I shall treasure it always.'

'Good. Now, you'd better go if you don't want to miss your train. Goodbye,' she said, and held out a hand to him imperiously.

'Well, I call that cool!' he exclaimed. He ignored the hand and pulled her into his arms.

'I was trying to be dignified,' she said when she could finally speak. 'And now you've ruined it.'

'I do beg your pardon, but I'm afraid I lack your sang-froid. I refuse to be dignified when we're saying goodbye.'

'I rather wish you hadn't come back at all,' she said. 'Now I shall have to forget you all over again.'

'But I don't want you to forget me,' he said. 'In fact, I shall be awfully offended if you do.'

She laughed.

'You know I couldn't possibly,' she said. 'Not really.'

'I don't suppose you'd like to come with me?' he said lightly after a moment.

'No, Edgar, I don't think I would.'

'I didn't really expect you to say yes, but I thought it couldn't hurt to ask,' he said.

'Well, I thank you for the kind thought, but I'm quite happy here,' said Angela.

'Yes, I can see that,' he said. 'It would be selfish of me to drag you away even if you wanted to come. It's just that now I've got you I'm finding it rather a wrench to let you go.'

He tightened his arms about her as he spoke.

'It would never work,' she said. 'There's no sense in even thinking about it.'

'I dare say you're right,' he said. 'I'm sorry.'

'So am I.'

'I'd like to have met you under different circumstances,' he said. 'But as you've so rightly told me before, I chose my path and now I have to live with it. Shall you ever approve of me, do you think?'

'I don't know,' she said. 'Perhaps one day. Go and do something splendid and we'll see.'

'Such as what?'

'Oh, I don't know. You might slay a dragon, or—or save somebody's life, or perform some act of glorious self-sacrifice. That ought to do the trick.'

'I'm not sure I like the sound of that,' he said. 'Perhaps I shall have to content myself with struggling to live an honest life.'

'That will be admirable. I wish you all the best with it.' she said. She freed herself with some difficulty. 'Now go, and don't come back.'

'I won't promise,' he said.

'I shouldn't believe you if you did,' she said.

He kissed her one last time and a second later was gone. Angela watched out of the window as he got into his car and drove off into the damp November morning, then turned away. She was trying very hard to be sensible about things. There was no use in regretting him, for there had never been any hope to start with and she was not one to indulge in useless wishing. No; it was much better this way. They had parted on the best of terms and now at least she could remember him fondly and with a smile. She could not say whether his attempt to pursue the straight and narrow path would be successful, but if it were not she was unlikely ever to find out about it and be disappointed. Now all that remained was for her to be firm with herself and suppress any awkward feelings for him that might remain. She was confident of her own strength and was certain it would not take too long.

She stifled a yawn, for it had been a long night. It was not quite seven o'clock, however, and she had no plans for Sunday, so she decided that there was no harm in trying to get a few hours' sleep. She was heading towards her bedroom when she caught sight of something out of the corner of her eye and turned her head to glance at it. It seemed to be a shoe, and it was protruding from behind the sofa at a very strange angle.

'How odd,' thought Angela, and paused. She looked at it more closely, still not understanding what it was she had seen. Then realization stole across her and she froze. For several seconds she stood there, quite immobile, while her heart began to beat rapidly. At last she took a deep breath and approached the sofa very slowly, although she already knew perfectly well what she would find, for she had seen it often in the past— often enough, certainly, to recognize it when she saw it.

There it was, just as she had known it would be: the body of Davie Marchmont, lying behind the sofa in a pool of blood, barely recognizable—although who else could it be? Briefly, she knelt down by him and reached out for his wrist as though to look for a pulse, but then in an instant she drew back, for of course there was no pulse; a single glance at him was enough to tell that. She stood up again and moved away and for a long moment stared down at him—at the thing which had once been her husband. Anyone observing her would have said that she was in shock—and perhaps she was, although it had not deprived her of the ability to think, for her mind was working rapidly.

At length she turned away from him, went into the bedroom and changed from her evening-dress into day clothes. The police would be here soon, and it would not do to greet them in silk and pearls. Then, after a moment's thought, she went over to her bed and pulled the covers back. When she was ready, she returned to the sitting-room and lifted the telephone-receiver to call Scotland Yard. After that, she sat down in a chair to wait. Angela Marchmont was by no means a stupid woman. She had no idea what her husband was doing in her flat or who had killed him, but one thing she did know was that she was in very great trouble.

61

CHAPTER SEVEN

M RS. MARCHMONT?' SAID Sergeant Willis of Scotland Yard. 'Are you quite sure, sir?'

'Of course I'm sure,' said Inspector Scott tetchily, still holding the telephone-receiver in his hand. 'Do you take me for an idiot?'

'No, sir,' said Willis.

'Well, then,' said Scott. 'I've never met the woman myself but I understand you know her. She says she found the body this morning. It's her husband, apparently.'

Inspector Scott was a compactly-built man of middle height and thinning hair, whose disposition was not improved by a tendency to dyspepsia. Sergeant Willis respected his abilities but found him slightly hard to take by comparison with the even-tempered Inspector Jameson, who was away on honeymoon at present. Scott also had an unfortunate love of writing reports, and Willis (who did *not* love writing reports) had been most put out at having been summoned to work early on a Sunday morning to catch up on his record-keeping. He had got no further than filling in his name at the top of a page, however, when a call had come in to say that a Mrs. Angela Marchmont had found a dead body in her flat. This was surprise enough, but the identity of the dead man was even more unexpected.

'I didn't even know she had a husband,' said Willis.

'Well, she hasn't any more, by the sound of it,' said Scott callously. 'We'd better get over there now and take a look before she has a chance to tamper with the evidence.'

'Why should she do that?' said Willis.

'Any number of reasons,' said Scott. 'She's the one who plays at being a detective, isn't she? Fancies herself cleverer than the police. By the time we get there she'll probably have pocketed half the evidence so we can't deduce anything from the scene of the crime.'

'She doesn't usually do that,' said Willis. 'She's always been very respectful, as a matter of fact.'

'Well, and what of it?' said Scott. 'Because there's always the other possibility, which is that she did away with him herself. She's probably scrubbing the house clean of clues as we speak.'

He stood up and strode towards the door.

'Or she might even be upset at the death of her husband,' said Willis quietly to himself, as he followed his superior out of the office and down the stairs.

But despite the kind-hearted Willis's supposition, Mrs. Marchmont showed no signs of being particularly upset at her husband's death when Scott and Willis arrived. On the contrary, she looked a little pale and tired but perfectly composed.

'He's behind the sofa. I haven't touched him,' was the first thing she said as she admitted them to the flat.

The two policemen walked over to look at the mortal remains of Davie Marchmont. It was not a pleasant sight. It looked as though he had taken a shot to the head, but the bullet had not passed through cleanly, for there was a certain degree of mess. Sergeant Willis winced. Inspector Scott turned to Mrs. Marchmont, who had remained at the other side of the room, presumably not wishing to look at the body again.

'Did you say you found him here this morning?' he said.

'Yes,' said Angela.

'Do you have any idea what happened?'

'No.'

She seemed unwilling to elaborate.

'When did you last see your husband? Alive, I mean,' said Scott.

'It was on Thursday,' said Mrs. Marchmont. 'Here, at my flat. We talked, then he went away again. I believe he was staying at Burkett's.'

'Staying at Burkett's?' echoed the inspector. 'Didn't he live here?'

'My husband and I were separated,' said Angela. 'He's an American and he usually lives—lived—in New York. I hadn't seen him in more than two years when he arrived on Wednesday.'

'I see,' said Scott, in whose mind ideas were turning over rapidly. 'Why did he come to London?'

'I don't know,' said Angela, then corrected herself. 'Or rather, I know he came to me for money. Whether that was his sole purpose in coming to England I couldn't tell you.'

'He wanted money? Did you give him any?'

'Yes, I did,' said Angela.

'May I ask how much?'

Angela hesitated, then went over to her writing-desk, brought out of a drawer her cheque-book and handed it to him. Scott looked at the sum written on the most recent counterfoil and just managed to stop himself from whistling. He made no comment, however, and merely handed back the cheque-book.

'Thank you,' he said. 'Now, if you don't mind I'd like you to tell me more about what happened. At what time did your husband arrive?'

'I've no idea,' said Angela. 'I was out last night, at a charity ball. He certainly wasn't here when I left the flat, though.'

'And at what time did you arrive home?'

'I left the ball not long after midnight and came home in a taxi. I was back by twenty past twelve,' said Angela. This was just the first of many lies she would tell over the next weeks, but it was by no means the worst.

'And was he here then?' said Inspector Scott.

'I don't know. I suppose he must have been.'

'Do you mean you didn't see him?'

'No. I'd had a little to drink and I was tired, and I wasn't thinking of anything much. I certainly had no reason to look behind the sofa before I went to bed, which is why I didn't see him until this morning.'

'Was the front door locked when you arrived home last night?'

'Yes. Yes, it was,' said Angela reluctantly, after a moment's hesitation.

'Then how did he get in?'

'I think he had a key. My maid is away for a few days, and before she went she left her key on the table there. After Davie visited I noticed it had gone and I assumed he'd taken it.'

'But why should he do that?' said Scott.

'I don't know. Perhaps he did it accidentally or absent-mindedly,' said Angela. She was careful not to accuse him of anything deliberate for she was fully aware, even at this early stage, of how important it was not to display any sign of outright hostility towards her dead husband.

Inspector Scott was an able enough man, but he was not the sort to go looking for difficulties where none apparently existed, and he had already pretty much made up his mind on this case.

'Mrs. Marchmont, do you have any idea who killed your husband?' he said.

'No,' said Angela. 'My first thought when I saw him was that he had killed himself.' She wanted to add, 'Just to spite me,' but thought better of it.

'But there's no gun. If he'd killed himself then there would be a gun next to the body.'

'I know,' she said.

'You didn't happen to see a gun when you found your husband?' said Scott. 'And pick it up, perhaps?'

'No.'

'Are you quite certain of that? You might have done it absent-mindedly or accidentally, just as your husband did with your keys.'

The inspector's manner was bland, and he seemed to be offering her a way out, but she would not fall into the trap.

'No,' she said. 'I hardly went near him. I certainly didn't pick anything up.'

She looked up, saw Sergeant Willis hovering sympathetically in the background, and felt a little sorry for him, for they had always been on friendly terms and she imagined that he was feeling somewhat torn at present. As if in confirmation of her supposition, he offered her a half-smile and then turned away, looking uncomfortable. Inspector Scott had no such qualms, however.

'Mrs. Marchmont, were you and your husband on good terms?' he said abruptly.

'We weren't the best of friends, certainly,' she replied. 'That's why we parted company. However, there was no particular animosity between us. We tolerated one another and were on civil terms, at least.'

Another lie. This one was slightly easier to tell than the first, and Angela was thankful that her arms were covered so that the bruises did not show.

'Why did you give him money?'

'Because he said he needed it,' said Angela. 'He was still my husband, after all.'

'Didn't he work?'

'He found it difficult to hold down a job,' said Angela shortly.

'Are you sure that's the only reason you gave him the money? He didn't threaten you, for example?'

'Of course not,' said Angela. 'I told you, we were on civil terms. He asked for the money and I gave it to him. I could afford it, after all.' Here she only just managed to keep the bitterness out of her tone.

'Do you own a gun?' said Inspector Scott.

This was a facer, but after a moment's reflection Angela decided that there was no sense in lying about it, since it was a matter of public record.

'Yes, I do,' she said.

'Where is it?'

'I keep it in the second drawer of that chest by the window,' she said.

Scott nodded to Willis, who went to the chest, wrapped his hand in a handkerchief and carefully opened the second drawer.

'It's not there,' he said.

'Are you sure?' said Angela. Now that she had determined on her course, it was becoming easier all the time to act the part. 'Try the other drawers.'

But of course the chest of drawers contained no gun.

'Might you have put it somewhere else?' said Scott. His manner was becoming increasingly polite as his conviction of her guilt became more assured.

'No,' she said. 'I always kept it there. Do you suppose the murderer took it?'

'Perhaps,' said Scott non-committally. As a matter of fact, he was half-inclined to arrest her there and then, but the lack of a weapon posed something of a difficulty. There was no doubt at all in his mind that Angela Marchmont had shot and killed her husband, but it would be difficult to prove that until they had found the gun. No doubt she had disposed of it somewhere, and he could only hope she had hidden it in the flat. The place would have to be searched, of course, and more evidence collected, but as far as Scott could see, it was an open-and-shut case.

Just then, the doorbell rang and suddenly the room was full of men with bags and cases and stretchers, who saw that the bereaved wife was present and so lowered their voices, trod carefully on the expensive Persian rugs, and tried not to knock into the furniture. Angela did her best to stay out of the way as they worked. She had remained calm so far, but it was partly out of a sense of disbelief at events, for it was perfectly obvious to her what was about to happen, and among all the confusion the one thing that stood out in her mind was a burning sense of resentment at her husband who, she was irrationally convinced, had done this deliberately to get her into trouble, for she could not think of a more perfect crime. The locked door, the missing weapon, the evidence of the cheque-book—all of this together painted a clear picture of a woman who had taken a gun and shot dead her husband in a fit of rage. And why should anyone think differently? It looked very much to

Angela as though the police had a water-tight case against her. She had left the house at about nine o'clock the night before and (as far as the police knew) had returned just after midnight. At some time between nine and a quarter to seven that morning, Davie had come to the flat for reasons best known to himself, and had been shot dead. Unless it could be proved that Angela was out of the house when he was killed, then she would be arrested for his murder. But what if it turned out that he had died after midnight? Then she would have no alibi at all, for she could not—would not—confess where she had really been. That was quite impossible. No, the police must continue to think that she had spent the night at home, and she could only hope that the medical evidence would show that Davie had died before midnight, when several witnesses could confirm that she had been at the White Rabbit Ball. Perhaps it would even turn out that the gun which was used to kill Davie was not hers. But how could that be proved? There was no other weapon here, and she had, of course, given her own revolver to Edgar Valencourt, who was presumably on his way to France at this very minute. She had no way of sending a message to him, for she had no idea where he was going, and even if she had, he was unlikely to come forward with the gun, since he would be arrested immediately himself if he did. Despite all the things he had said, she did not suppose for a moment that his interest in her extended to getting himself into trouble. No, there was certainly no help to be expected from that quarter. The gun was gone and with it a vital piece of evidence.

At that moment she could see no way out, and a sense of defeat came upon her. She supposed that Davie had always meant to do her a bad turn in whatever way he could, although this was the last thing she had expected. Oddly, in the whirl of her thoughts she did not pause to wonder who really had killed her husband, for it did not seem to matter much. After all, why would the police bother looking for anyone else when they had a perfect suspect right before their eyes? She looked across to the other side of the room, where the police were working, and found Inspector Scott regarding her thoughtfully. He withdrew his gaze immediately but there was no doubt at all what he had been thinking. Angela turned away and stared at the wall. At that moment she felt more alone than she had ever done before.

CHAPTER EIGHT

THE DOCTOR SOON pronounced it to be his considered opinion that David Marchmont had died at some time between eight o'clock on Saturday night and two o'clock on Sunday morning, and that death had occurred as a result of a gunshot to the head—most likely from a small-calibre weapon of some sort, perhaps a revolver. It then became a matter of some urgency to find the murder weapon. A search of Angela Marchmont's flat was instituted, but turned up nothing. However, other evidence of some interest was unearthed. Firstly, the little chest of drawers in which Mrs. Marchmont claimed to have kept her revolver was tested for finger-prints, and the results indicated that only she had touched it. Secondly, a search of Mr. Marchmont's body revealed that he was not in possession of a key to the door of his wife's flat, which suggested strongly that Mrs. Marchmont had let him in herself. On questioning, Mrs. Marchmont stated that she had no idea what had happened to her maid's key, but guessed that perhaps the murderer had taken it. Be that as it may, it was certain that the key was missing and nobody knew where it might be. It was also remarked during the search of Davie's pockets that he was carrying three gloves: one pair in tan suède and an odd one in dark grey. It was assumed, however, that he had lost the other grey glove and had forgotten to take its mate out of his pocket before coming out, and the fact was quickly forgotten.

The search of the flat continued for most of the day, and all the while Angela sat quietly, keeping out of everyone's way and saying nothing unless asked a question by the police. Her husband's remains were removed, along with a number of her personal effects, and still the search went on. At about three o'clock one of the men gave a sudden grunt of satisfaction, and announced that he had found the bullet. It had embedded itself into the wall next to a large painting, and there was some activity while they tried to get it out. Eventually it was removed, and the men congratulated one another at having retrieved it more or less undamaged. The same could not be said of the wall, however, which was now quite ruined. Angela considered saying something about it, but then decided against it, for it seemed to her that a hole in the plaster-work was quite the least of her worries.

Meanwhile, Sergeant Willis had been sent out to question the other people who lived in the building. Most of them had been out for all or part of the evening, but of the ones who preferred to remain at home on a Saturday night none had seen or heard Davie Marchmont arrive—for this was not the sort of building in which one neighbour spied on another, being inhabited mostly by wealthy people who were far too pleased with themselves and their own concerns to trouble their heads over what their fellow residents were doing at any given moment. Willis did manage to establish, however, that a number of loud bangs had been heard over the course of the evening, including several after midnight. Given that it was only a few days after the fifth of November, everyone had assumed that the noise was youngsters letting off fireworks, and had disregarded it as nothing more than a nuisance. According to one irate elderly woman, there had been one particularly loud bang just after ten, which was so loud that it almost seemed as though it had gone off in the building itself. Inspector Scott disregarded this when he heard it, since Mrs. Marchmont claimed to have an alibi for that time. Instead he concentrated his attention on the bangs that had been heard after midnight, for it seemed most likely that one of them had been the shot that killed Davie Marchmont.

After Willis had got all the information he could out of the other residents and reported back to Inspector Scott, the two men stood on the landing outside the flat and conversed in low voices. Mrs. Marchmont was inside, under the watchful eye of a police constable, although she seemed to have no intention of trying to make a run for it.

'So, then,' said Scott. 'It's all looking clear enough. Mrs. Marchmont comes home from this ball—incidentally, we'll have to talk to the people she was with to confirm she was there at all. Still, let's assume she was. She's just got home when her husband turns up for a late-night visit, having already dunned her for money and made a nuisance of himself earlier in the week. They have a row—she says herself that she'd had a bit to drink—and she gets the gun out of the drawer and shoots him. Then she panics, disposes of the gun and calls us.'

'After presumably going to bed and getting a good night's sleep first,' Willis could not help pointing out. 'She didn't call us until this morning, and her bed looked as though it had been slept in.'

'It's easy enough to rumple up a bed,' said Scott dismissively.

'But why did she wait so long before she called us?'

'Who knows?' said Scott. 'Perhaps she spent the whole night looking for somewhere to dispose of the gun.'

'Easy enough to get rid of a heavy object in London,' said Willis. 'You just drop it in the Thames.'

'I expect that's what she did in the end,' said Scott. 'But who's to say how long it took her to come up with that idea? I don't suppose she was thinking straight. Or perhaps I'm wrong—perhaps she's just cold-hearted and callous enough to have got rid of the gun immediately and come home again. Perhaps she slept the sleep of the just all night while her husband lay in a pool of blood on the parquet in the next room.'

Willis opened his mouth to argue but closed it again. He was a good policeman and knew that he must not let his liking for Mrs. Marchmont obscure the facts, which, he had to admit, all pointed to her guilt.

'I wonder what the money was for,' went on Scott thoughtfully. 'It was a tidy sum. I wonder whether he mightn't have been blackmailing her. We'll have to look into that. Something like that would be a big enough motive for murder.'

'But she'd already paid him,' said Willis.

'Yes, but we don't know whether he'd already cashed the cheque,' said Scott. 'Perhaps she decided to put him out of the way before he could do it. Or perhaps he'd come to ask her for more money. That's the trouble with blackmailers: they never know when to stop. It might be that he pushed her a little too far, and she decided to put an end to it once and for all. I dare say it will all come out when we look more deeply into the thing. So, then,' he went on, with a cheerfulness that was entirely misplaced, in Willis's view, 'I suppose we'd better take the lady in. I only wish all cases were as easy as this one. If we hurry, we can get back to the Yard and finish those reports by the end of the day.'

Willis thought of Inspector Jameson, away in Scotland with his new wife, and wished he had been the one to take the call. But no, he corrected himself; the Jamesons were friends of the chief suspect, and the inspector would never be allowed to investigate this case. Willis wondered what he would say when he found out what had happened. It was likely to be a shock to everyone, he thought.

The two men entered the flat and found Angela Marchmont and the police constable both sitting in silence. The other men had packed up and left, and but for the bloodstains behind the sofa and the hole in the wall one would never have known that a violent death had occurred here. Mrs. Marchmont looked up expectantly and showed no surprise as Scott announced that he was arresting her on suspicion of the murder of her husband and gave her the usual warnings.

'Of course,' she said. 'I didn't do it, but I quite understand why you have to arrest me.'

She stood up and accepted the coat and hat that Sergeant Willis brought her. He still looked very uncomfortable.

'I'm sorry,' she said to him, and meant it sincerely.

She took one last glance around the flat—it would be some time before she saw it again—and then the four of them left together and descended to the police-car that was waiting for them outside. As they drove off it began to rain again.

CHAPTER NINE

MR. ADDISON, OF Addison, Addison and Gouch, sat at the bare wooden table and tried his best not to look uncomfortable, although his chair was hard and he was generously built and he was worried that he might not be doing a very good job of it. He shifted slightly and glanced at his notebook.

'I am glad you agree with our choice of defence counsel,' he said to his client, Angela Marchmont, who was sitting at the other side of the table. 'Mr. Travers is the very best there is. He could not be here today as he is in court for the poisoning case, but he has asked me to assure you that he believes there to be several weak points in the prosecution's argument, and he will come to see you to discuss them as soon as he is able.'

'I look forward to seeing him,' said Mrs. Marchmont. 'I have met Mr. Travers once or twice in company and have always judged him to be a most capable man. I shall be interested to hear what he has to say.'

Angela was bearing up to the indignities of incarceration as well as might be expected in the circumstances, and was as politely interested as possible in what Mr. Addison was telling her, but in reality she had assumed the worst almost from the moment she had found her husband's body. Even she had to admit that all the evidence pointed to her being the murderer, and more than once, in the middle of the cold, dark night, she had reached such a low pass as to wonder whether perhaps she *had* done it while in the grip of some sort of brainstorm, and had somehow forgotten it afterwards. Of course, she knew logically that whoever had killed Davie Marchmont, it was not she, and outwardly she tried to remain brisk and optimistic that some evidence would emerge to prove her innocence, but deep down she was racked by pangs of guilt over the lies she had told the police, and she could not silence the murmurings of the small voice in her head which told her repeatedly that she deserved everything she got.

Of all the incredible things about the case, it seemed to her that the *most* incredible was the fact that the only person who might give her an alibi for the fatal hour was the one man whose help she could not request, for he was far away—who knew where?—and to whom she had no means of sending a message. But even if she could somehow manage to get word to him, then what could he be expected to do? Present himself and confess cheerfully that at the fatal time the two of them had been driving into Kent to return a ruby brooch he had stolen to its rightful owner? Why, the very idea was absurd! And how would the court look upon her association with a notorious jewel-thief? She could hardly suppose that they would view it favourably, for, as she herself had to admit, most people would quite rightly say that there was no innocent reason at all for a married woman—even one separated from her husband—to spend the night in the company of a known criminal. Even though her intentions had been good, the whole incident appeared distinctly fishy and was likely to make her look even more guilty than she already did, since the proper thing to do, of course, would have been to report Valencourt to the police. Although, as she had said, she considered herself free of her husband following their separation, it was unlikely that the man in the street would find anything to approve of in her friendship (if so it could be called) with Edgar Valencourt—indeed, she did not particularly approve of it herself and had done her best to fight against it, albeit with mixed success. But leaving aside all selfish considerations, there still remained one thing above all which meant she would never be induced to speak, and that was the fact that her sense of honour would not allow her to break a promise and give Valencourt away. He had told her that he was going to try and give up his old ways, but whether that were true or not did not matter. They had had an understanding, and that being so she could not betray him, even to save herself.

Still, she could not help but kick herself at her insistence on giving him her gun. She had no idea whether or not her revolver was the weapon which had killed her husband, but had she not given the thing to Valencourt then it might have proved her innocence in one way or another. For example, if the gun could be produced then the bullets inside it could be examined. If they were different from the one which had killed

Davie, then that would indicate that some other weapon had been used, and, by implication, that someone else had done the deed. If, on the other hand, it turned out that her gun *was* the weapon which had been used to kill him, then someone else's finger-prints would presumably be on it, again pointing to her innocence. But all the vital evidence had now been destroyed, for she had herself taken the gun out of the drawer and given it to him, and now both their finger-prints would be on it. That being so, perhaps it was better that the gun was now safely out of the way, for who knew what conclusions might be drawn if it were produced now?

Mr Addison was speaking again, and Angela forced her attention back to the present.

'I beg your pardon,' she said. 'You said something about Freddy?'

'I said that Mr. Pilkington-Soames has asked me to pass on his regards. We have every reason to be grateful to him, for he has been working tirelessly to find witnesses to support our case.'

'It's terribly kind of him,' said Angela dutifully.

'It is. As he said, it is cheaper than employing a private detective, and as a reporter he is in a position to ask questions that others may find difficult to countenance. I am glad, now, that we agreed to let him look into the matter. There is no doubt at this point that we need some help on our side, for the police believe they have a strong enough case and so they are not inclined to look too hard for any other evidence, but there are a few leads we should like to follow. For example, we are trying to find the boys who were presumably letting off fireworks on the night of your husband's death. If it can be demonstrated that all the explosions which were heard after midnight were in fact made by fireworks, then that may go some way towards strengthening your case, for it will at least imply that the shot was fired before midnight—a time for which, of course, you have an alibi.'

'It doesn't sound like much,' said Angela.

'No, but every little helps, as they say, and if we can find enough small pieces of evidence, we may be able to build them into a solid case for the defence. Don't forget, the jury must find you guilty "beyond reasonable doubt." Our task is to introduce that doubt into their minds and thus force them to acquit you.'

'I see,' said Angela.

Mr. Addison puffed up a little with excitement, for he had been saving a piece of news.

'By the way, I think you will be very pleased when you hear of another witness your friend has found,' he said.

'Oh?'

'Yes. As a matter of fact, he has spoken to someone who claims he saw a man threatening your husband on the steps of Burkett's on the very day of the murder.'

Here he paused to observe the effect of his words. Angela looked duly impressed and invited him to continue.

'Yes,' he went on. 'You may remember I told you that a person had come forward and told the police that he had something of importance to say about the case. Scotland Yard took down his story but disregarded it, for they do not consider the man to be a reliable witness, as he is already known to them. He is one Josiah McLeod, of no fixed abode, and he spends most of his days standing outside the clubs of St. James's, where he ekes out a small living from the generosity of the clubs' patrons. Mr. Pilkington-Soames brought the man to me, and we both agree that he tells a most interesting tale. According to his story, he was outside Burkett's at about four o'clock on the Saturday afternoon in question when he saw two men emerge from the building in conversation, one of whom was Mr. Marchmont. He knew your husband's name because he knows most of the members of the club by sight, and he had remarked upon the appearance only a few days earlier of an unfamiliar face—one, moreover, with an American accent—so he had been paying particular attention and had soon overheard the commissionaire address him as Mr. Marchmont. Jos did not know the other man at all, and could only say that he was youngish and smartly dressed. He also said that there was something slightly foreign about him, although he was unable to explain what he meant by that; it was certainly not the man's accent, which was an English one. It is not a particularly helpful description, but I am afraid it is the only one we have.'

'Go on,' said Angela in sudden interest.

'According to Jos, the men appeared to be having some kind of altercation, although he was unable to hear exactly what it was about. As he describes it, the second man said something in a low voice to Mr. Marchmont, who heard him with a sort of incredulous smile upon his face and made some scornful reply. They were just walking down the steps then, and Jos says he distinctly heard the foreign-looking man say, "I won't dirty my hands trying. I shall simply shoot you as I would a dog."'

'Goodness me,' said Angela, in whose mind an awful thought was forming. She quickly quashed it and inquired, 'And what did Davie say to that?'

'He was not given the opportunity to reply, for the other man then walked away.'

'I see,' said Angela.

Mr. Addison was a little disappointed. He had expected his client to be more excited at this sensational new evidence, and could not help saying so.

'Of course, Jos is hardly the most reliable of witnesses,' he said, 'but we shall clean him up and make sure he stays sober, and I am confident that he will do well in court.'

'Oh, I have no doubt of it,' said Angela. 'Of course, this is an extremely valuable piece of evidence, and I'm tremendously grateful to Freddy for finding this fellow. I don't mean to be a pessimist—it's just that I rather fear we won't be able to find the man who is supposed to have threatened Davie at the club. If he is a foreigner, then perhaps he has already gone back to wherever he came from.'

'Well, young Freddy is going to speak to the people at Burkett's to see if anyone can shed any light on the man's identity,' said Mr. Addison. 'Let us hope he is successful.'

'Yes, let's,' said Angela. 'Excuse me, but are you sure this Jos has no better description to give of the second man? He cannot say whether he was tall or short, for example? "Youngish, with something slightly foreign about him" is not exactly helpful.'

'I believe his exact words were that the man was "a smart-looking gent, a bit too got up to be English,"' said Mr. Addison.

'I am afraid that Jos is not particularly known for his sobriety during the day, so the fact that we have got even this much out of him is a small miracle. He did say, however, that he thought the man might have dropped something, for he saw your husband bend down and pick up an object from the steps shortly after the other had left. That might mean anything or nothing, though. It was most likely something your husband had dropped himself.'

'Then you think it might have been this man Jos saw on the steps who killed Davie?'

'Perhaps, but whether it was or not does not matter. As I have said, our main concern is to put a doubt in the minds of the jury as to whether *you* did it. As a matter of fact, I intend to speak to Mr. Travers on this subject as soon as possible. He may be of the opinion that it is better not to search too hard for this man, for if it turns out that he did not kill your husband, then we are back where we started.'

'Yes, I see what you mean,' said Angela. Of course, she could not tell Mr. Addison what she was really thinking, for she had the most dreadful suspicion that the man seen with Davie outside Burkett's was in fact Edgar Valencourt. It would be quite astonishing if it were so, but according to this Jos, the altercation had taken place at around four o'clock, not long after she had met Valencourt in Hyde Park, and she could not help but remember the furious look on Valencourt's face when he had seen the bruises on her arms, although he had said little at the time. What if he had taken it upon himself to go and warn Davie off? She would never have supposed him to be the type to threaten people, for he had always said that he preferred to avoid all that sort of unpleasantness. However, she knew from her own encounters with him that he disliked violence against women, and perhaps he had enough feelings for her—or at least was angry enough on her behalf—to go and speak to her husband when he found out that she had been hurt.

But what an idiotic thing for him to do, if he had indeed done it! Why, he might easily have aroused Davie's suspicions against them even further—although, on second thoughts, perhaps he believed it did not matter, since he was intending to leave the country the next day. Angela did not know whether to be appalled or pleased at the thought of what Valencourt might have done. Her dealings with her husband were none of his business, and it was sheer arrogance on his part that he felt he had the right to threaten Davie, for of course he had no right at all. Still, though, she could not suppress a flutter at the thought of his caring enough about her to do it. But surely he could not possibly have meant what he said about shooting Davie. What a terrible coincidence that he should have said such a thing, given what had happened only a few hours later!

She spent several hours after Mr. Addison had left turning the matter over in her mind, and became more and more convinced that Edgar Valencourt was the man who had been seen on the steps with Davie. Of course he would never be found, for he was far away now and had probably taken good care to hide his traces, but perhaps Jos's story would be enough to convince a jury that Angela was not the only possible suspect in the case, and would be sufficient to induce them to acquit her. The thought gave her some comfort—of which she had felt little up to now. If Valencourt could not be there in person to give her an alibi, then he might at least be able to save her this way. It was only a very slight possibility, but at present it was the only hope she had.

CHAPTER TEN

NOW, MRS. MARCHMONT,' said Mr. Travers. 'If we are to secure an acquittal, it is of the utmost importance that you tell me everything you can about your relations with your late husband. You understand that you must not hide anything, however damaging you believe it might be to your case—in fact, the more damaging you believe it to be, the more important it is that you tell me of it, for if the prosecution were to catch us by surprise, then that could easily ruin things completely. Let me be quite clear; I do not want to hear vital information for the first time in court. If you know anything, then you must tell me now.'

The poisoning case was finished, and Mr. Travers had won yet another victory (although privately he was certain that his client was guilty), and he was now ready to devote his full attention to Mrs. Marchmont's case. Percival Travers, K.C, was one of the finest legal minds in the country, and had made a great reputation in his thirty or more years at the Bar. Very early in his career he had shown a decided talent for defending the most hopeless of cases, and it had become something of a point of pride with him over the years to add to his tally of successes—for as he never tired of saying, it was easy enough to point at a poor soul who was already wretched and miserable at having spent a month or two in prison and convince a jury that he was guilty, but it was not so easy to plant enough doubt in the jury's mind as to the wretch's guilt that they would be prepared to acquit him. He had been only too keen to represent Angela, for they had met once or twice in the past, and although he thought the case would be a difficult one, he had defended worse, and successfully, too, as he pointed out. He now smiled encouragingly at Angela in his most avuncular manner.

'Very well,' said Angela hesitantly. 'What is it you wish to know?'

'Let us start from the beginning. When did you first meet your husband?'

'I don't know exactly,' said Angela. 'It must have been about fifteen years ago, shortly after I first went out to America.'

'You worked for many years, I believe?'

'Yes. I was employed by the Duke of Lewes as personal secretary to his wife when I met Carey Bernstein, the American financier, who took a liking to me and asked me to come and work for him in New York instead. I had always rather wanted to travel abroad, and so I said yes. Davie was a relation of Mr. Bernstein's wife—her sister's son, and I met him very soon after I arrived in America. That was before the war.'

'You did not marry him then?'

'No,' said Angela. 'We married a few years later, in early nineteen seventeen.'

'And was the marriage a success to start with?'

'No. I realized very quickly that I had made a mistake,' said Angela shortly.

'In what way?'

Angela hesitated. Mr. Travers peered at her over his spectacles.

'Remember, you must tell me everything,' he said.

Angela had always hated talking about personal matters, but she knew he was right, of course. This was no time to keep things to herself. She gritted her teeth and went on.

'I worked for Mr. Bernstein for five years and in that time became his most trusted employee. He was very rich and owned many companies, most of which he had built up himself. He was particularly astute in the matter of investments—the buying and selling of stocks and bonds and so forth—and he taught me a great deal about it. He was kind enough to say that I had a better mind for picking investments than any man he had ever met, and after a few years he surprised me by putting me in sole charge of a small stockbroking firm he owned, Bernstein & Associates. He told me the job would be very difficult, because many people would refuse to deal with a woman, but he was willing to try me out and see what I was made of. He was right, of course; the early years were very hard, and there were many occasions on which I was convinced I had failed and thought of giving it up. But somehow I stuck with it, and eventually I started to make the place a success, and soon the company was bringing in more money than it had ever done before, and people stopped worrying about the fact that I was a woman—mostly, at least—and were happy to deal with me because they saw that I knew what I was doing.

'When Mr. Bernstein died in nineteen sixteen he left me some money and a fifty per cent share in the firm. I think he would have liked to leave the whole thing to me, but his family were horrified at the very idea, and so in the end he gave in to them and left me only half. He left the other half to Davie—I believe at the urging of his wife, since they had no children themselves, and Mrs. Bernstein thought of Davie almost as a son.

'Davie and I married a few months afterwards, but I regretted it almost immediately. He had always been very charming to me but I had never thought seriously about him, and had it not been for the fact that I was feeling rather low at the time I don't think I should have accepted him.'

'Why did you regret it?'

'Because I quickly realized that his purpose in marrying me was merely to get his hands on more money. Davie had no head for business at all, and certainly no inclination to work, but he knew I had made Bernstein & Associates a success in only a few years, and he thought I should provide him with an easy income. And of course I did,' she went on bitterly. 'Within a year he'd spent all the money Mr. Bernstein had left me, and was draining the company of cash as fast as he could. I saw well enough what was going to happen and in the end I bought him out at a premium. I had to go into debt to do it, but I didn't want to see all my past efforts in making the company a success go to waste, and I was certain I could pay it off very soon if I worked as hard as I possibly could. It took me nearly five years to pay it off, but I did it. Of course, Davie had spent what I paid him for his share of the company long before that, and kept on coming back for more. I suppose it was all the same to him whether he had an interest in the firm or not, since he knew he could rely on me to supply him with anything he wanted.'

'Dear me,' said Mr. Travers. 'But you did not apply for a separation when it first became clear to you that the marriage was not a success?'

'No,' said Angela. 'Oddly enough, I took the view that if one makes a vow then one ought to keep it as far as possible. Davie had no such scruples, though.'

'Do you mean there were other women?'

'Yes, and plenty of them,' said Angela. 'He had no shame at all in flaunting them in front of me. For a long time I thought I must be the one at fault, and so I did my best to please him. It was perfectly useless, though, and in the end all I could do was to try and ignore his unfaithfulness as much as possible. Oh, listen to me,' she said in sudden distaste. 'How I despise myself for complaining like this. Look here, Mr. Travers, I should hate you to think of me as some feeble little wife, wringing her hands helplessly while all this was going on. I assure you I was nothing of the sort. I was a grown woman when I accepted Davie and it was my mistake to make. Of course the marriage didn't work, but I might have escaped from it whenever I chose. It was partly my pride that prevented me. I've never grumbled about it because I've always rather taken the view that one must play the hand one's dealt, and for a long time I was very good at that. In the end it was too much, and I came back to England to get away from him, but I won't be painted as a victim. Davie's arrival in London was an annoyance to me but nothing more. When he turned up at my flat I decided that enough was enough, and that I would divorce him as soon as I got the opportunity, but that's all. I disliked him and wanted him to leave me alone, but I didn't murder him.'

'Excellent,' said Mr. Travers. 'And as a matter of fact, you have put your finger on the very thing that is most important in the affair. It would be a grave error for us to try and paint you as a victim of an unpleasant husband, for that would give the jury the idea that you had a strong motive to kill him. Motive does not make a case but it must be a very independent-minded jury indeed that fails to be swayed by it, and of course the peculiar circumstances of your husband's death make it all the more important to play down any apparent animosity between the two of you.'

'I know that very well,' said Angela. 'It's just rather unfortunate that we disliked one another so much.'

'You must not mention that,' said Mr. Travers. 'Now, then, we come to Mr. Marchmont's unexpected appearance in London. I understand from the police that you gave him a cheque for a rather large sum of money.'

'Yes, I did,' said Angela.

'Why is that?' said Mr. Travers.

'Why, to get rid of him,' said Angela. 'I wanted him to go away.'

'But five hundred pounds? That is an enormous sum. And I understand that that constituted most of the money you had in your bank account at the time.'

Angela opened her mouth to reply, but Mr. Travers went on:

'Mrs. Marchmont, you must understand the way a jury's mind works. Of course, you are perfectly aware that under the law a person is considered innocent until proven guilty. Now, it is my unpleasant duty to tell you that whatever the law says, this is pure nonsense. The very fact of your appearing in court accused of a crime creates an unintentional presupposition that you are guilty—for if you were innocent, then why should you be there at all? That is what people think, and that is why it can be very difficult to secure an acquittal once a case has come to court, for the jury is already half-convinced that the person before them is guilty of the crime for which he is being tried. It is unfortunate, but it is the best system we have at present, and this is what you are battling against. Now, then, if a jury hears that you have been writing cheques for five hundred pounds and giving them to people you dislike—for the fact of your estrangement from your husband indicates that you were no longer on good terms—they will immediately wonder why you did it. And in this sort of case, the first word that is likely to spring into their minds is "blackmail."'

He paused and looked at her earnestly.

'Mrs. Marchmont, was your husband blackmailing you?'

Angela hesitated. She had never thought of it in those terms.

'I shouldn't call it blackmail, exactly,' she said reluctantly at last.

'Ah,' said Mr. Travers. 'I thought so. Then he knew something to your disadvantage and was threatening to disclose it? Did he have evidence of another man, perhaps? I beg your pardon, but I must ask these questions.'

'No, he had no evidence of anything like that,' replied Angela with exact truth.

'Then what is it? What have you not told me? Did anybody else know of it? Is it something which is likely to come out in court? I understand the prosecution intends to produce one or two witnesses from the United States, including your husband's mother.'

Angela looked up sharply.

'Della?' she said in dismay. This was bad news. Davie's mother had always heartily disliked Angela, and if she were intending to give evidence against her daughter-in-law then that meant only one thing: it would certainly all come out now.

'You had better tell me,' said Mr. Travers gently.

There was no getting out of it. Angela hesitated, then took a deep breath and told him the thing she had not wanted people to know.

CHAPTER ELEVEN

THE NEWS OF Angela Marchmont's arrest for the murder of her husband took all her friends and acquaintances completely by surprise. Many of them had not been aware that she *had* a husband, and even those who knew it were astonished at the idea of the mild-tempered Angela's taking a gun to anybody in anger. Perhaps the most shocked of all was Freddy Pilkington-Soames, who, having seen Angela only the night before her husband's death, could not quite believe what had happened after her sudden disappearance from the White Rabbit Ball. His immediate thought was that the man he had seen dancing with Angela must have been her husband, but as soon as he read a description of the dead man he knew that it was not so, for Davie Marchmont had been fair-haired and stood at more than six feet tall, whereas the man at the ball was dark and not more than about five feet eleven. Furthermore, Davie had not been wearing evening clothes when he was found. Who was the other man, then?

Had this been a story on which he was reporting for the *Clarion*, in which the principals were personally unknown to him, Freddy, that most suspicious of young men, would immediately have assumed that the lady and the gentleman had been in it together; that they had left the ball and gone back to the lady's flat, whereupon they had unexpectedly encountered her husband, with all too tragic consequences. But this was his friend Angela Marchmont, and cynic as he was, he would not believe it of her. She was not the sort of person to involve herself in sordid doings of this kind, he was sure of it. Perhaps the man he had seen at the ball was a mere acquaintance of Angela's. But no; a few minutes' reflection was enough to tell him that he had not been mistaken in what he saw. There had been something between them—that was clear enough—but surely it had no connection to this Marchmont fellow's death? Freddy was certain that Angela had not shot anybody, but might this man have done it? Again, though, that did not sound like Angela, for he could not believe that she would lie to protect a murderer, whatever her feelings for him might be. It was a mystery, and one that had put Angela in peril of her life, for the police did not seem to be looking for anyone else in connection with the affair. If another suspect could not be found, then Angela would be tried, found guilty and hanged, Freddy was almost certain of it.

He was determined to help, and so as soon as he could he volunteered his services as a detective to Mr. Addison. The solicitor was doubtful at first, but Freddy was insistent and in the end Mr. Addison agreed to ask his client whether she would consent to it. Angela did not believe there was much

Freddy could do, but recognized the expression of friendship that lay behind the offer and was grateful for it, for she had been uncertain how people would take the news of her arrest. The young man had many leads he wanted to pursue, said the solicitor, and it certainly could not do any harm to let him try. Angela agreed, therefore, and Freddy set to his task.

It was the work of only a day or two to speak to the police and trace Josiah McLeod, whose evidence sounded most promising despite his unprepossessing appearance. Unlike Angela, however, Freddy did not make the connection in his mind between the man at the ball and the man on the steps of Burkett's, for he had fastened too strongly upon Jos's description of the latter as foreign-looking, and was imagining someone of far less English appearance than Edgar Valencourt. Freddy thought that the man on the steps might be someone with whom Davie Marchmont had fallen out (for, from the little he had heard of Angela's husband, he seemed the sort of chap who fell out with everyone sooner or later), and hoped that *if* more evidence of this row could be found, and *if* it could be proved that Angela had not been at home on the night of the murder, then she would be cleared.

The only flaw in this line of reasoning was that Angela had stated quite firmly to the police that she had spent that Saturday night in her flat. Of course, if she had indeed been somewhere she ought not to have been, then this was only to be expected—in the early stages of the investigation, at least, but it seemed rather odd to Freddy that although they were now at the point of planning her defence for the trial, she was still apparently clinging to her original statement. However carefully he put the question to Mr. Addison or Mr. Travers, they still seemed to think that she had no alibi for the period after midnight on the night of the murder. That presumably meant Angela was telling the truth about where she had spent the night—either that or she had not told her lawyers where she had really been, for some reason of her own. Freddy reflected long and hard on this. Of course, he had no proof at all that she had not done exactly as she said on the night of the ball, but it was not like her to go home early without saying goodbye—and, furthermore, it was *most* unlike her to fail to spot a dead body lying in her own flat. Why, she had made a reputation for herself as a detective precisely because of her keen powers of observation. It was almost unthinkable that she should have missed the sight of her husband lying dead in a pool of blood for nearly seven hours! No, the more he thought about it, the more certain Freddy became that Angela might have a perfectly good alibi if she chose to use it, but that up to now she had chosen *not* to use it. This would not do; evidently the shock of being arrested had affected her powers of thinking in some way, for it was quite absurd of her to risk her life over her reputation. If she would not admit to it, then it was up to him to find the evidence that would prove where she had been that night.

His first thought was to ask the other members of the party whether any of them had seen Angela with a man that night, but somehow he could not bring himself to do it, for he knew she would hate it if she found out that they had been talking about her in this way. His next idea was to search quietly for the taxi driver who was supposed to have taken her home shortly after midnight, for he had the suspicion that the man had carried more than just Angela in his cab, and that they had not gone to her flat. But again Freddy was uncomfortable at the idea of doing this, for he felt that it was somehow furtive and underhand. In the end, he decided that before he started his investigation he would give Angela the opportunity to tell him about it herself, and then only if she denied everything would he take matters into his own hands.

So it was that he found himself sitting in the uncomfortable chair opposite Angela, who had reluctantly agreed to allow him to visit her in prison, although she had at first insisted that she did not want to see anyone. The atmosphere was stiff for the first few minutes; she replied shortly to his inquiries after her health, and looked altogether as though she would rather be elsewhere.

'You're looking a little thin,' he said at last. 'Aren't you eating? I dare say the food isn't up to much here.'

'No, it isn't,' she replied. 'The foie gras is quite dreadful, and I had to send the smoked salmon back the other day because it was starting to curl at the edges.'

'That's more like it,' said Freddy. 'I knew you were in there somewhere.'

'Somewhere, perhaps,' said Angela. 'I'm not certain there's much of me left.'

'Cheer up, old girl!' he said. 'We'll get you off, you'll see. I have lots of tricks up my sleeve.'

'I wish I could believe it, Freddy,' she said, 'but it all looks rather hopeless from where I'm sitting.'

'Well, yes, everything's bound to look hopeless when you have to sit on these chairs. Did someone design them with the express purpose of causing numbness to the average human posterior within the space of five minutes or less, do you suppose?'

She did not laugh, and he regarded her sympathetically.

'Listen, Angela,' he said. 'I wanted to talk to you seriously without all these overbearing lawyer chaps present. As a friend, you understand. I want to help you so very much, but it's difficult when you're not telling the whole truth to people.'

'What do you mean?' she said. 'Of course I'm telling the truth.'

'Well, yes, in some respects I expect you are,' he said. 'But why are you keeping quiet about this man of yours?'

He observed her closely as he said it, and had to admit to himself that she carried it off very well, with merely the slightest flicker of the eyelids.

'What are you talking about?' she said. 'Which man?'

'Why, the man I saw you with at the White Rabbit Ball. You were dancing and making the most awful sheep's eyes at one another when you thought nobody was looking.'

'I danced with lots of men that night, Freddy,' she said with apparent carelessness, although inwardly she was aghast at how easily she had been seen through. 'And I can assure you I didn't make sheep's eyes at any of them.'

'But I saw you,' said Freddy. 'I was struck by it at the time, and I was making up my mind to tease you about it when I saw you next. But then this all happened and I never had the opportunity. I never shall now, because it's suddenly become far more important than just a silly joke. You must see that. I should hate to think of your being found guilty of something you didn't do just because you're trying to protect someone who probably doesn't deserve it.'

For a moment he looked like a worried little boy, and she was touched by his concern. Could she have told she might have done it then, but of course she could not.

'I do see it,' she said, 'and I wish I could say anything different, but I can't. Do you really think I'd be sitting here now if I had a handy alibi? I assume that's what you mean, at any rate: you think I wasn't at home that night, but I can assure you I was, just as I said. I don't know which man you're talking about. I danced with quite a few that night, and I dare say I flirted with one or two of them, as one does when one's enjoying oneself. Then I came home and went straight to bed, and rather stupidly didn't spot until the next morning that someone had killed my husband and left his body behind the sofa.'

'Oh, Angela,' said Freddy sadly, for he did not believe a word of it.

There was a silence, and she looked down at her hands.

'Besides, don't you think it would look even worse if there *were* someone?' she said quietly. 'I still shouldn't have an alibi because they'd just think we were in it together—that we'd both killed Davie. Then they wouldn't call me only a murderer, but other things besides.'

For a second her lips trembled, and Freddy regarded her with the greatest pity. He was now certain that his guess had been right, and was privately disgusted at the man, whoever he might be, for not coming forward and giving her an alibi. Presumably he was married and had a position to maintain, and would let Angela hang rather than get himself into trouble. Angela was an honourable woman and would not give him away, but any true gentleman would have stepped in immediately to save her. Freddy resolved there and then that he would find this man if at all possible, and force him to do what he ought.

'Angela—' he began.

'Listen, Freddy,' she said in a firmer voice. 'I promise you that if there were anything I could possibly do to make them let me out, then I should do it—should have done it long ago, in fact. I'm in the most awful fix, I know that, and I'm tremendously grateful that you've done as much as you have for me, but please don't feel bad if things don't—turn out well.'

'You mustn't think like that,' he said. 'Of course things will turn out well. We'll find out who really did it and they'll acquit you and let you go with a handshake and an apology, and perhaps even a bouquet—' here she did manage a smile, '—and we'll forget any of this ever happened.'

'I hope so,' she said. 'But how can we find out who did do it?'

'I only wish I knew,' he said. 'It's a pity you can't do any investigating yourself, stuck in here. But I shall do what I can, if you'll only tell me where to start. I mean to say, you must have plenty of spare time here to think about things. Have you come to any conclusions as to who might have murdered your husband?'

'Well it must have been someone he knew,' she said. 'I imagine I wasn't the only person to find him tiresome. I don't know who would have had a big enough grudge against him to kill him, though.'

'Did he have friends in England?'

'Well, there was the man he was staying with at Burkett's. I can't remember his name, but I dare say you could find it out. I don't know about anyone else. As far as I knew, he had none.'

'But what was he doing in your flat?' said Freddy. 'Surely that's the oddest part of this whole thing. Why did he come?'

'I've no idea,' said Angela. 'I've thought and thought about it, but I don't know why he should have come when he did. He'd visited twice and asked for money, but it was a Saturday night, and he could hardly expect me to be at home—as a matter of fact, I'm fairly sure I mentioned to him that I should be out that night.'

'Perhaps he came deliberately, knowing you would be out,' said Freddy.

'Yes, I'd thought of that,' said Angela. 'He'd made various threats about—things, and I rather wonder whether he hadn't come to search my flat while I was at the ball.'

'Search it for what?'

'Evidence of another man, I expect. You're not the only person to accuse me of it. I made some mention of divorce and he didn't take it kindly. There is no such evidence, of course, but he wasn't to know that.'

'That makes sense,' said Freddy. 'Let's take it as a logical hypothesis, since he's not here to speak for himself and contradict us. So, then, let's say he was here to rifle through your escritoire and disarrange the silverware. What happened between his arrival and his departure, so to speak? Did he make so much noise opening and closing drawers that he attracted the ire of one of your neighbours, who turned up with a gun and dealt with the problem in summary fashion? I know there's little in this world that's more infuriating than someone rattling about in the next room when one's trying to sleep.'

'I doubt it,' said Angela. 'Most of the people in the building are old dears who can't hear a thing one says unless one shouts.'

'Well, in that case whoever did it must have arrived in company with your husband—otherwise they wouldn't have been able to get in through the front door downstairs.'

'I hadn't thought of that,' said Angela, 'but of course you're right.'

'But who was it? Might it have been this friend of his at the club you mentioned? I don't suppose he's been asked to provide an alibi. I shall have to look into that.'

'Do,' said Angela, who for the first time was starting to take an interest. 'He might have asked the friend to come and help him search my place.'

'Yes, that seems possible. All right, then, we have our first suspect. Now, what about others? You say you don't know of any other friends he might have had. Did he have family here?'

'No,' said Angela. 'I expect there's a woman somewhere, though. Davie always had a woman in tow. I never knew him to be without one.'

'Oh, one of those types, was he?' said Freddy sympathetically. 'Poor you. He must have worked fast, though, to secure himself a willing female only a day or two after his arrival. Didn't you say he'd only got here the day before he first turned up at your flat?'

'That's what he said, yes,' said Angela, thinking. 'As a matter of fact, Freddy, I wonder whether you mightn't be on to something. Of course it's too soon even for Davie to have picked someone up in the time, but he might have brought someone with him. Perhaps they came over together from New York. How can we find out?'

'Well, I imagine the first step will be to take a look at the passenger lists,' said Freddy.

'Will you do that? I'd do it myself, naturally, but I'm engaged for the foreseeable future.'

'No sooner said than done,' said Freddy, pleased to see that his friend was looking more alive and much more like herself at the prospect of these new leads. 'I shall go and bother the personnel at the White Star offices and refuse to leave until they give me what I want.'

'Splendid,' said Angela. 'I don't know how you might find out a name, but I'm sure you'll think of something.'

'I only hope so,' said Freddy under his breath as he left the prison shortly afterwards. It was a slim chance, but anything was better than nothing at this stage, and he was determined to do everything he could to get Angela acquitted of the charge against her.

CHAPTER TWELVE

FREDDY'S FIRST ACT on leaving the prison was to find a public telephone box, from where he called the offices of the *Clarion* to tell them that he had been struck down by a ghastly illness that might well prove fatal, and that as a consequence he would not be able to come in for a few days. Having convinced his editor that if he turned up to work he would most likely pass on scarlet fever, malaria, influenza and smallpox to everyone in the office, much to the disadvantage of the publication as a whole, he hung up and fished out his notebook, in which he had written a list, as follows:

1. Taxi driver
2. White Rabbit Ball party. Who saw the man?
3. Chap at Burkett's
4. Who was the woman? White Star. Where was she staying in London?

He frowned as he regarded the third and fourth points. It was not much to go on, but if they were right in their supposition that Davie had come to Angela's flat in company with his killer—and it seemed likely that this were the case—then it was vital that he find out more about Davie's movements in the days leading up to his death. Angela's revolver had still not been found, and until it was they should never know whether it was the weapon which had killed Davie, or whether another gun entirely had been used. The second set of door keys was also still missing. If either or both of those things could be found in someone's possession, then Angela would be in the clear. The police were not interested, and Angela of course could do nothing, so it was all up to him.

His eye then fell on points 1. and 2. of the list, which related to Angela's alibi. For the first time Freddy was struck by the absurdity of his determination to force an alibi on to someone who did not want it. Still, if he could find it then she should accept it whether she liked it or not. He was musing on this when an idea struck him, and he was surprised that he had not thought of it before. He took his pencil and added to the list:

5. Marthe

Of course Marthe would know who Angela's mysterious man was, if anyone did. He would speak to her immediately. She was a little frosty, true, but she adored her mistress and Freddy was confident that she would speak if Angela's life was at stake.

He hailed a taxi and shortly afterwards was set down at 23 Mount Street. Marthe was there, and regarded him suspi-

ciously through a crack in the door, but when he told her that
he was investigating Angela's case on her behalf she unbent
a little and stood back to let him in. He could not help but
glance about as he entered Angela's spacious, well-appointed sitting-room. There, facing him, was the sofa behind which Davie
had presumably met his end. It was a large chesterfield in green
leather, and it was placed facing the door with enough space
between it and the window to allow someone to pass behind it.

'Do you mind if I have a look?' he said to Marthe.

She shrugged and he walked over to it and gazed at the spot
where Davie Marchmont had lain. Of course, everything had
been cleaned up now, and there was nothing at all to be seen.

'What was he doing behind the sofa?' he said. 'It seems an
odd sort of place to stand, don't you think?'

'I have no idea,' replied Marthe. 'I do not understand anything. It is all quite absurd.'

'Perhaps he wanted to look out of the window,' he said,
'although there wouldn't be much to see in the middle of
the night.' He gazed about him. 'I take it the place has been
searched. And I expect you've had a good look around yourself
too, haven't you, Marthe?'

She said nothing, but merely regarded him politely with
eyebrows raised, as though waiting for him to tell her what he
would like to drink.

'You would tell me, wouldn't you, if you'd found any evidence?' he said, although he knew from Angela that Marthe
was something of a law unto herself. He had no doubt that if
she had found anything to her mistress's disadvantage then she
would have destroyed it immediately.

'Naturally,' said Marthe.

They gazed at one another in silence, Freddy wondering how best to approach the subject he really wanted to discuss. In the end he decided to come straight out with it.

'Listen, Marthe,' he said. 'I'm sure you want Angela to be released as much as I do, so you must tell me everything you know. It's terribly important that you don't keep secrets at a time like this. I need as much information as I can find out if I'm going to prove her innocence.'

'I understand,' said Marthe.

'Then I should like you to tell me about the man I saw dancing with Angela on the night of the ball,' he said. 'They looked as though they were on rather close terms. I believe she was not here at all at the time of the murder, but was somewhere else with this fellow, and she won't give him away.'

'But *monsieur*, I was not here on the night of the ball,' said Marthe. 'I know nothing of whom she danced with.'

This was prevarication at its finest, and Freddy had the sinking feeling that he should get nothing out of her.

'That's not what I meant, and you know it,' he said.

'Yes, I know very well what you meant,' said Marthe. 'And I tell you, there was no-one.'

'Please, Marthe,' said Freddy.

Was it his imagination, or did a look of pity briefly pass across her face? She would not give way, however, for she was absolutely loyal to her mistress.

'I have received a letter from Madame herself,' she said. 'She has assured me that she did not shoot her husband, and that she is absolutely certain that nobody of her acquaintance did it either, so I am not to worry myself about it.'

Freddy stared at her in puzzlement. Why on earth should Angela have taken pains to assure her maid that none of her friends had killed Davie Marchmont? Then it struck him: of course, it was a warning to Marthe not to give away the man! Angela could not risk saying it plainly, but she had as good as told the girl not to reveal his identity to anybody, for he had had nothing to do with the murder.

At that moment Freddy could have given Angela a good shake for her stubbornness in shielding this man. She was an intelligent woman, and had been perfectly right when she said that any alibi he provided was likely to be looked upon with suspicion by a jury, but still, he might be able to provide some proof of their having been elsewhere that night even if she could not.

For a second, Freddy found his faith in his friend shaken. If she was so determined not to reveal the man's identity, might that be because she was not, in fact, innocent? Might she have committed the murder after all? It was a brief jolt, but it soon passed and he was restored to all his usual optimism. Angela was not a murderer. Very well; if Marthe would say nothing, then he should find it out in some other way.

He left 23 Mount Street and walked a little way until he reached the mews where Angela's chauffeur, William, lived with the Bentley. If Marthe would say nothing then Freddy had little hope that William would be any more forthcoming, but he was determined to try, at least. Alas, his supposition proved correct, for William merely fixed him with a fierce stare and said that there was no use in Freddy's asking him anything, for he had nothing to say and would never speak ill of his employer or give away any information that might have been entrusted to him in confidence. At that point, Freddy gave it up and left, marvelling that Angela had managed to find two such unswervingly loyal servants—even if their loyalty was something of a trial to him at present.

His next stop was Burkett's club in Pall Mall, where after a few minutes' negotiation with the commissionaire, who regarded him askance, he was admitted and asked if they had seen Mr. Alfred Pearson that day. Mr. Pearson was there at that very moment, as it happened, and on hearing that a gentleman (the word was pronounced by the secretary with only a fraction of a second's hesitation) wished to speak to him in connection with the death of his friend Mr. Marchmont, declared himself only too happy to talk to the fellow. Police, was it?

Pearson was slightly taken aback when, instead of a police sergeant, he found himself face to face with a young man wearing an insouciant air and a slightly disreputable appearance. He was half-inclined to go back on his agreement, but Freddy was perfectly polite and respectful and so he hesitated and eventually invited the young man into the library, where they might converse in private.

'So you're here on behalf of Marchmont's wife, eh?' he said when they were seated. 'I gather they've arrested her for his murder. Terrible business, what?'

'It certainly is,' said Freddy. 'I know she didn't do it, but I'm having the devil of a job finding out who did.'

He had judged that the best approach was to be quite open with the man, for it would be difficult in the circumstances to question him without revealing what he was really looking for. If Alfred Pearson were the man they wanted, then he would be put on his guard, but that could not be helped. Still, Freddy's first impression of the fellow was that he did not seem the type, for he was a bluff, open-faced sort with the air of one eager to please. He did not seem the kind of person to have a friend like Davie Marchmont, and Freddy wondered how the two of them had met. Pearson soon explained.

'I'm awfully sorry the man's dead, of course,' he said, 'but I should be lying if I said we were close pals. I met him when I was out in New York on business a couple of years ago. Got lost in a down-at-heel part of town late at night. I had my evening things on, and a couple of toughs started to give me some trouble, but then Marchmont came along and sent them packing. He thought it was a tremendous joke and took me off for a drink to recover my nerves, then he took it upon himself to act as my tour guide for the rest of my stay. Very kind of him, of course, but the sorts of places he visited weren't the kind to appeal to me, since they all seemed to be illegal drinking dens—can't remember what they call them—some odd name. I won't say no to a drink or two myself, of course, but I was in New York on important business, and it wouldn't have done to get myself arrested, so I was pretty nervous all the while I was with him, and I wasn't sorry when I had to leave.

'I'd given him my address in Aldershot and told him to look me up if he was ever in England, although of course, that's the kind of thing one says. It doesn't mean anything, and I never really expected he would turn up. But then I got a letter from him to say that he was coming over to London for a little while, and could I put him up? I wasn't too keen on the idea, to be perfectly frank. I didn't think my wife would take to him much, and truth to tell I hadn't told her about those drinking dens in New York either. I was rather worried that he'd come out with the whole thing, and then I'd be in trouble. So instead of inviting him to Aldershot, I suggested that we stay for a few days at my club instead. He was all for that—he'd heard of these gentleman's clubs, he said, and he'd like to have the opportunity to visit one. So that's what we did. He arrived on the sixth of November—of course, you'll already know that from the police—and came to stay at Burkett's with me for a few days.'

'Was he alone?' said Freddy. 'I mean, he didn't have a woman with him at all?'

'Of course not,' said Pearson uncomprehendingly. 'Burkett's doesn't allow women.'

'No, but I thought you might have seen him in company with one outside the club.'

'No, no, nothing of the sort,' said Pearson. 'I never met his wife. In fact, he never mentioned her at all. That's why I was so surprised when I heard what had happened.'

Freddy gave it up, for it was perfectly evident that Pearson was an unsuspicious type who did not go around looking for bad behaviour in others.

'So, then,' he said. 'You were in company with him from Tuesday the sixth until Saturday the tenth of November. Did you see anything in that time which might have indicated that he had an enemy?'

'No,' said Pearson. He looked a little uncomfortable. 'As a matter of fact, though, I didn't spend all the time in company with him, since by that time I'd rather realized that he wasn't my sort of man at all, and so I'd begun to try and avoid him wherever possible.'

'Oh? Why was that?'

'Why, to start with the fellow never liked to pay his way,' said Pearson. 'Ducking out like that simply isn't done, but he seemed to expect that I would cover all his expenses. You know, his bills here at the club and suchlike. He was playing cards one evening and he borrowed some money off me for that, too. I assumed he'd pay me back, but after a day or two he still hadn't done it and I thought I'd better say something. I remarked upon it jokingly and he said something about settling up later, but when I reminded him of it the next day he laughed and said he'd thought I wouldn't expect it of him, given the obligation I was under for his having saved me in New York that time. I thought that was rather a low thing to say, and I was so surprised at it that I said so. That just made him laugh all the more. Then he clapped me on the shoulder and said he was a little short of funds and he knew I wouldn't mind subbing him while he was here, because we were pals, weren't we? After all, we both knew I could rely on him not to mention anything to my wife about what we'd got up to in those drinking places in New York.'

He paused, a worried expression on his face.

'That sounds rather like blackmail to me,' said Freddy.

'It does, doesn't it?' said Pearson. 'And yet I never thought of it in that way at the time—I mean to say, he never said outright that I'd better pay for him or he'd tell my wife—but I did feel uncomfortably as though I had better watch my step. At any rate, I stopped mentioning the money and tried to distance myself a little from him for the next day or two. Of course, I couldn't go home to Aldershot as I'd spoken for him at the club, but I said something about going to visit an old friend of mine who was sick, which gave me an excuse to get away for a day. He didn't seem to mind—said he could amuse himself easily enough while I was away.'

'What day was that?' said Freddy.

'That was the Saturday,' said Pearson.

'The day he died?'

'Yes.'

'Then you never saw him again?' said Freddy.

'Yes, I saw him again,' said Pearson. 'I returned early that evening and found him at the club, playing cards with some of the chaps.'

'And how did he seem then?'

'Oh, tremendously cheerful. He always had a smile on his face, you know. Nothing ever seemed to put him out. He greeted me as though he hadn't noticed that I'd been trying to avoid him—although I'm certain he must have—and invited me to sit down and join in the game. I didn't want to give him any more money and was about to refuse when he threw a bundle of notes at me and said it was by way of repayment, and that he'd had a stroke of good fortune and was feeling rather flush at present. He was intending to return to New York in the next day or two, he said, and I'd soon be rid of him. He must have seen me hesitate because he said, "Come on, old fellow. I've thrown down the gauntlet and you can't say no." Then he laughed uproariously as though he'd said something enormously funny, and kept on urging me until in the end I agreed to join in. There didn't seem any harm in it—especially as he was paying his own way now and was going to leave soon. To be perfectly frank, it was idiotic of him to play that evening. He'd quite obviously been drinking, but he didn't seem to care about the amount of money he was losing.'

'Did he lose a lot, then?' said Freddy, thinking of the five hundred pounds that Angela had given her husband only a few days earlier, thrown away in a drunken card game.

'Oh, yes,' said Pearson. 'He seemed to be very much in funds that evening. I pointed out to him that perhaps he ought to give it up before he lost it all, but he just said I needn't worry— that there was plenty more where that came from, and he was going to get it very soon. Then he said "I'm going to throw down the gauntlet again, Pearson, and then I'll be set for life." He seemed to think the remark was hilarious, although I haven't the faintest idea why.'

'People get odd ideas when they're drunk,' said Freddy.

'I suppose so,' said Pearson. 'At any rate, he didn't have the chance to lose all his money, because eventually he looked at

THE SCANDAL AT 23 MOUNT STREET

his watch and said he had to leave, as he had arranged to be elsewhere.'

'At what time was this?' said Freddy.

'Nine o'clock, or thereabouts. That's what I told the police, at any rate. I can't remember to the exact minute, of course.'

'And he didn't give you any clue as to where he was going?'

'None at all,' said Pearson. 'But now I realize he must have gone to see his wife. Strange, isn't it? I mean, I didn't know him especially well, but one would have thought he'd have mentioned being married, don't you think?'

'They were separated,' said Freddy.

'Ah, is that it?' said Pearson. 'Sad when that happens. It goes on too much these days, and I don't like to see it. Still, if they weren't on good terms I suppose it explains why she killed him. I don't like to speak ill of a man when he's dead, but he wasn't quite the thing, you know.'

'Yes, and that's the problem,' murmured Freddy. It was all too easy to see why Angela might have taken a gun to Davie Marchmont. What he needed was a reason why she had *not*. Pearson's story had given him little new information, although one part of it was certainly suggestive. Davie had left the club at about nine and gone somewhere else—and not in the company of Pearson, by the sound of it. But where had Davie gone? No-one had come forward to say that they had seen him after nine o'clock, and so the police had naturally reached the conclusion that he had gone straight to Mount Street. Angela herself had said that she thought Davie might have wanted to search the flat while she was out, but if the police's theory were the correct one, and Davie had died after midnight, then that meant he had spent three hours there until Angela came home. Surely it would not have taken him three hours to search the place? It seemed improbable that he had been there all that time. But if he had gone somewhere else before going to Mount Street, then where? And with whom? There must have been someone with him, surely—and perhaps that person had gone with him to Angela's flat. This was not much, and was certainly unlikely to impress a jury, but it did seem to be a point in Angela's favour.

Freddy thanked Mr. Pearson and left the club, then walked the short distance from Pall Mall to the White Star offices, where a representative of that company greeted him cheerfully and listened to Freddy's heartfelt and completely fictitious story of an elderly uncle of reduced understanding and his entanglement with a gold-digging American chorus-girl. A secret marriage was suspected, and there was the matter of an inheritance, upon which a most virtuous and deserving family had been relying to save them from a life of poverty and humiliation. Freddy gave a most affecting performance as he described the travails of the family in question, who had accepted their lot patiently and without complaint. It was of the utmost importance, he said, that they find out one way or the other whether a marriage had indeed taken place in the United States, for the principals would not or could not speak, and the only way of finding out seemed to be to consult the White Star passenger lists, since a trip to America was quite out of the question.

Whether or not the company representative believed him cannot be said, but evidently Freddy made a good enough impression that he very soon found himself examining the passenger lists of the *Homeric* for early November. There in the first class column he soon found Davie Marchmont, who, as was only to be expected, was not listed as travelling with a wife—although Freddy had half-hoped that if there *were* a woman she might have travelled under his name. He then looked at the few single women's names. They meant nothing to him but he took them down anyway. Then it struck him that, from what he had heard of Davie Marchmont, she was just as likely to have sailed second class—although on second thoughts perhaps not, since then they would have been kept apart during the passage, and Angela had said that Davie always liked to have a woman on hand.

Freddy chewed his lip in thought. What he really needed was to speak to one of the stewards who had been on that voyage, and who remembered Davie and could tell Freddy whether he had spent any time in company with a woman while on board ship. The cheerful White Star representative was hovering helpfully nearby, and Freddy made his request. The representative's face fell. He was sorry, he said, but the *Homeric* had departed that very morning for New York, with all its usual crew on board (as far as he knew), and was not expected back for over two weeks.

This was a blow. Angela's trial was due to begin in ten days, and Freddy had hoped to have some solid evidence to present long before then. He took a note of the *Homeric's* expected date of arrival, then thanked the man and left the offices. It looked as though he had reached a dead end with respect to that particular line of inquiry, at least for the present, although he was determined to speak to someone from the crew as soon as the ship docked. In the meantime, he would carry on with his investigation as best he could, however hopeless the case was now looking.

CHAPTER THIRTEEN

THE TRIAL OF Mrs. Angela Marchmont for the murder of her husband promised to be the greatest of *causes célèbres*. Not since the arrest of Dr. Crippen had the British public felt such pleasurable anticipation at the thought of the sensation which could be expected from the event, for rumours had emerged of scandalous behaviour on all sides, and there was nothing the man in the street liked better than the sight of high society conducting itself shamefully. Mrs. Marchmont was, of course, already well known for her exploits in the field of amateur detection, and all recognized and appreciated the grim irony that now placed this woman, who had brought several murderers to justice, in the dock, charged with the very thing she had always fought against. All wanted to see the spectacle of a famous society lady being forced to answer for herself—for although there was no particular bad feeling towards her on the part of the public, there was perhaps a tinge of malicious glee at the thought of seeing her in the very position in which she had placed so many others with apparently so little thought.

It was a grim day in early January when the trial began, and so great was the curiosity to witness the event that a queue of people began to form outside the Old Bailey from quite early in the morning. By the time the doors opened, the queue stretched almost as far as Newgate Street and one or two scuffles had broken out, which immediately came to an end as soon as the crowd began to move forward. Once inside, it was a race to secure the best seats, and there was a certain amount of bickering and shoving until everyone was settled.

Freddy Pilkington-Soames had no need to queue at dawn, of course, for he was there representing the *Clarion*, that shining beacon of truth and reason, as he liked to call it when in particularly jocular mood. He arrived at the last possible minute and sauntered down to the press bench, accompanied by a woman with fair hair and a worried expression.

'Shove along, Harry, will you?' said Freddy to the grizzled old man sitting at the end of the bench, who announced his credentials as a paid-up and long-suffering member of the Fourth Estate by means of one pencil behind each ear and three more sticking out of his top pocket. The old man began to protest, but Freddy ignored him, sat down at the end of the bench and forced everyone to shuffle up until there was room for his companion, who sat down likewise.

'Are you sure I'm supposed to sit here?' whispered Kathie Jameson. 'I'm not a reporter.'

'No, but we'll say you're here to take notes on behalf of Scotland Yard,' said Freddy. 'After all, it's almost true. We don't want old Jameson to miss anything, do we? Here, have a pencil.'

He plucked the aforesaid object from behind the ear of Harry and handed it to her. The old man protested again briefly then immediately filled the vacancy with another from his top pocket. Kathie dug out a scrap of paper from her handbag and glanced around guiltily.

'I wish Alec could be here,' she said.

'He has work to do and criminals to catch,' said Freddy. 'Not for him a life of ease, sitting in court idly watching the public dissection of friends.'

'Don't!' she exclaimed.

'Sorry, old girl,' he said. 'I'm as upset about it as you are, of course, but I can't help the black humour. It rather helps one get through things like this.'

'I do hope she's all right,' said Kathie.

'Of course she is,' said Freddy. 'And she will be. It's all rotten, but soon it'll be over and she'll be released and we can all go back to poking fun at one another.'

'I wish I could believe it,' said Kathie. 'But Alec says the case looks bad against her.'

'Well, she's got Percy on her side,' said Freddy. 'If anyone can get her off, he can. Perhaps he has a few tricks up his sleeve.' Just then, there was a commotion and a barked instruction to rise. 'Oh, and we're off. Up you get.'

Everyone rose to their feet as the judge and his acolytes filed in and made themselves comfortable. Then they all sat again and Kathie, whose eyes had been fixed on the bench, now turned her head and saw Angela standing in the dock, smartly dressed and very composed. She was perhaps a little thinner than before, and was certainly pale, but otherwise she looked as she always had. Mrs. Marchmont glanced briefly at the crowd she had drawn and then turned her attention towards the judge. Throughout the trial, she would maintain that same attitude of calm concentration, causing some to call her cold and unfeeling. For now, those in the public gallery contented themselves with examining her closely. Some whispered that she was taller than they had supposed, while others said she was shorter. Some said she wasn't as good-looking as she'd been made out to be, while still others said it was a shame for a woman to be so concerned with dressing elegantly when her husband was lying dead and cold in the ground. Fortunately, Angela was oblivious to all this, as was she to the curious glances that were darted at her by the members of the jury: ten men and two women, all of whom seemed extremely aware that they were taking part in an event of great importance, for they all had a certain air of self-consciousness about them, as though they had been asked to pass judgment on Queen Marie Antoinette or some other grand personage, instead of the rather ordinary woman before them who was accused of a domestic crime that was by no means terribly unusual. At any rate, their expressions seemed to say, at least this was likely to be interesting—far more interesting, in fact, than a mere case of burglary or fraud.

Then the murmur was hushed up and proceedings began. The judge gave his usual speech to the jury, who sat up and looked even more self-conscious, after which it was thought necessary to get the legal arguments out of the way. This was all very dull, and consisted of much to-ing and fro-ing between the defence and the prosecution on matters which were of minute interest to those in the know but which caused nothing but blank incomprehension on the part of everyone else. The attention of the spectators had just begun to drift away when there was a stentorian clearing of the throat, and a voice addressed one Angela Lillian Marchmont and invited her to speak. She was accused of the murder of her husband, David Alexander Marchmont, on the night of the tenth of November or early in the morning of the eleventh of November last. How did she plead?

'Not guilty,' said Angela, and everybody in the public gallery shuffled in pleasurable anticipation.

The floor was then thrown open to allow the prosecution to begin its case.

'I say, they've wheeled out the Attorney-General,' whispered Freddy to Kathie. 'Hasn't he got anything better to do?'

Sir Benjamin Hicks-Reddington, K.C.V.O, K.C, M.P, was a man of enormous importance—not least in his own eyes. In his many years at the Bar, he had successfully prosecuted and defended some of the most famous legal cases of modern times. Any soul who found himself in the unfortunate position of having to answer to a murder charge in court invariably breathed a sigh of relief and considered himself a lucky fellow on being informed that 'Redd' would be defending his case, for that gentleman was blessed with a brilliant legal mind, together with a sort of genius for spotting the flaw in any argument advanced by the other side. In addition to this, he was handsome, with a rich, resonant voice, which he used to great effect in his speeches, for he was also an orator of great talent and eloquence. Fortunately for those who might baulk at the idea of so much perfection unfairly concentrated in one human being, Sir Benjamin was also an exceedingly vain man. No-one could possibly be fonder of him than he was of himself, and nothing pleased him more than to catch sight of himself in some reflective surface—be it a looking-glass, a silver knife, or even a particularly shiny vase—and pause, as it were accidentally, to admire the sight out of the corner of his eye (for he was wise enough not to make the thing *too* obvious). Vanity aside, however, there was no getting around the fact that he was a formidable adversary, and Freddy's exclamation was prompted less by disrespect than by a stab of dismay that Angela now had a harder task ahead of her, for if it were a very good thing to have Sir Benjamin on one's side, it was a very *bad* thing to have him acting against one.

Sir Benjamin cleared his throat and began, and soon the entire court was in thrall to that rich voice as it addressed the jury.

'Ladies and gentlemen,' Sir Benjamin boomed, 'you are here today, not on behalf of any person in this court—neither the judge, nor the lawyers, nor the prisoner, nor the people in the public gallery—but on behalf of a man who cannot be here today for reasons quite outside his control. His name is—or was—David Marchmont, and he was the husband of the prisoner, Angela Marchmont, who is the woman you see before you. In the next few days, it will be your task to decide whether Mrs. Marchmont was or was not directly responsible for his death, and if the answer be yes, whether the killing was intentional or accidental. This is a weighty task that now falls upon your shoulders, and you must not shirk your duty, but instead must face it with courage, conviction and a clear head. As you bend your efforts towards the ends of justice, you must do so impartially, objectively, and without prejudice. You may, for example, have already heard of Mrs. Marchmont. There are few people in the land, I expect, who have *not* heard of her, for she has been a stalwart presence of late in the newspapers, which have dwelt much upon her exploits. There is no denying that she has gained a sound reputation as an amateur detective, and the men of Scotland Yard will be the first to admit that she has frequently given them valuable assistance, and on more than one occasion has been responsible for bringing dangerous criminals to justice. And yet despite this I tell you that you must now *forget* all you know of her; you must forget everything you have ever read about her in the popular press, for none of it is relevant to the instance at hand. The case upon which you have been called to pronounce judgment is a very simple matter, and can be summed up thus: did Angela Marchmont or did she not murder her husband? That is all you are required to decide; and how Mrs. Marchmont brought about the arrest of such-and-such a person, or what she said when such-and-such a criminal was caught, are of no interest to us at all at present. As his lordship has quite rightly told you, you must confine yourself to the facts of the case and forget everything else.'

'How he does go on. I wonder if he's paid by the word,' murmured Freddy to Kathie.

'Now,' went on Sir Benjamin, 'let us begin. Ladies and gentlemen of the jury, it is my intention to demonstrate to you beyond all possible doubt that Angela Marchmont did, with malice aforethought, take a gun and shoot her husband dead in the early hours of the morning on the eleventh of November, nineteen twenty-eight. I will demonstrate to you that the prisoner had every reason to kill her husband, that she had the means to kill him and that she had the opportunity to do it. Furthermore, from the witnesses I will produce you will hear that Mrs. Marchmont has no alibi for the fatal time; that is, she cannot prove that she was elsewhere at the moment her husband was shot.' He paused to let this sink in, then threw a hand out grandly and exclaimed, 'Let the first witness be called!'

The first witness was less impressive than might have been supposed from his introduction, being none other than Inspector Scott, who in a brisk voice described the circumstances under which the death of David Marchmont had come to his attention, and what the police had found when they arrived at Angela Marchmont's flat at 23 Mount Street.

'This flat is in a building with other flats, is it not?' said Sir Benjamin. 'Where is Mrs. Marchmont's flat located in relation to the others?'

'On the third, or top floor,' said Scott. 'There are four flats on each floor.'

'Is the building served by a lift?'

'Yes.'

'What about a porter?'

'There is a porter, but he was not there when we arrived, and I have since found out that his attendance is somewhat irregular,' said Scott.

'You have spoken to him, then?'

'Yes. He was away sick on the Saturday and Sunday in question and could tell us nothing about what had happened.'

'Very well,' said Sir Benjamin.

There followed questions on the location and position of the body when it was found, then Sir Benjamin said:

'Where was Mrs. Marchmont while you were conducting these investigations?'

'She was in the flat,' said Scott.

'Did you question her?'

'Yes. I asked her if she knew anything about what had happened to her husband.'

'And what did she tell you?'

Scott related what Angela had told him. The court listened attentively.

'And how did she appear to you? Did she seem at all upset at Mr. Marchmont's death?' said Sir Benjamin.

'Not especially,' replied Inspector Scott. 'In fact, she didn't seem upset at all. She was very calm all the time we were there.'

'Did this surprise you?'

'At first, but then she told us she had been separated from her husband for more than two years, which went some way to explaining it.'

'Then Mr. and Mrs. Marchmont were not on good terms?'

'That's not what she told us. She said that they were not the best of friends, but that they were civil to one another.'

The questions then moved on to the matter of the missing door key, after which everyone was left in no doubt that Mrs. Marchmont must have admitted her husband to the flat on the night of the murder, since he had not been found in possession of a key.

Sir Benjamin now invited the defence to cross-examine. Mr. Travers was as unlike Sir Benjamin as it was possible to be, being a mere wisp of a man by comparison with the Attorney-General, and yet there was something about him that held the attention. He now rose to his feet and addressed Inspector Scott. He was very curious to know whether the police had found any sort of weapon in the flat.

'No, we didn't,' said Inspector Scott. 'We searched the place thoroughly but there was no trace of a gun.'

'Did you ask the prisoner whether she owned a gun?'

'We did, sir, and she admitted that she owned a revolver.'

'Then how did she explain the fact that there was no gun in the flat?'

'She couldn't explain it. She said the murderer must have taken it.'

'I see. Then there is no clue at all as to the exact nature of the weapon which was used to shoot the prisoner's husband, is that correct?'

'Not exactly,' said Inspector Scott. 'When we were searching the flat we found a bullet embedded in the wall at such an angle as to make us pretty certain that it was the one that killed David Marchmont.'

The article in question was then produced and handed to the jury, who examined it with great outward solemnity and inward excitement.

Mr. Travers continued:

'But since we have no gun, we cannot be absolutely sure who owned the weapon that killed him, is that correct?'

Inspector Scott admitted that this was the case, and Mr. Travers sat down. He had attained his point, and had planted a doubt about the weapon in the minds of the jury. Freddy, however, happened to be looking at Sir Benjamin at that moment, and could not but remark the satisfied smile that now spread over the Attorney-General's face.

'Hey, hey,' he said to himself. 'I wonder what old Ben has up his sleeve now? He looks far too pleased with himself for it to be anything we want to hear.'

CHAPTER FOURTEEN

T HE NEXT WITNESS was the doctor who had first examined the body. He gave a dry little cough and repeated for the benefit of the court his view that David Marchmont had died some time between eight o'clock on the night of Saturday the tenth of November and two o'clock in the morning on Sunday the eleventh of November. He then proceeded to explain that it was never possible to be entirely certain about time of death, and went into some little detail about the temperature of the room and the state of the body when he had seen it with respect to the advancement of rigor mortis, much of which was not understood by the majority of his listeners. Still, the point had been made and the idea was firmly fixed in the mind of the jury that an alibi was needed for the period from eight o'clock until two o'clock.

The doctor's evidence concluded with his initial opinion on first seeing the dead man that he had been shot in the head, but he was given no opportunity to expand on this for he was then hustled off to be replaced by Dr. Everett Menzies, the well-known pathologist, who had performed the post-mortem examination on David Marchmont. The court sat up with interest at this, for Dr. Menzies had in the past few years made quite a name for himself in the field of criminal pathology, and had, thanks to his scholarly research and confident manner of giving evidence in court, sent a number of murderers to the gallows and exonerated several others.

Dr. Menzies was a tall, spare man with a tendency to regard people down his nose, which gave him a particularly arrogant look. As it happened this habit, which was purely physical, was not in the least bit misleading, for it matched perfectly his personality, since Dr. Menzies had never been known to countenance the mere possibility that he might be wrong about anything, and in fact was perfectly convinced that he represented a superior form of humanity. Fortunately for him, his abilities *almost* matched his opinion of himself, and so he and the law mostly got along very well indeed, and his was invariably the first name on everybody's lips whenever a case involving particularly tricky medical evidence presented itself.

In this case, however, the medical aspect was not particularly taxing. Dr. Menzies announced almost idly that according to his examination, David Marchmont had been killed by the passage of a projectile through his head. The bullet had entered the deceased's skull through the right temporal bone, just grazing the occipital bone as it did so, and had emerged through the left frontal bone. Asked to put it more simply, Menzies explained that the bullet had gone in just behind the right ear towards the base of the skull, had passed diagonally through the dead man's head and had emerged through the temple just above his left eyebrow. From the scorch marks on the entry wound, he continued, he judged that the shot had been fired at close range.

'Do you mean that whoever killed David Marchmont shot him from behind?' inquired Sir Benjamin.

'Not *exactly*,' said Menzies. 'I should say it was more to the side and just slightly behind.'

This was a distasteful thought, and a whisper set up in the public gallery as the spectators considered the new idea that Mrs. Marchmont had not killed her husband in a fit of rage after all, but had crept up on him and quite deliberately put a bullet in his brain. Any woman might lose her head and take a gun to a troublesome husband in the heat of a row, it was agreed, but a shot almost from behind was not fair play at all.

'Silence!' ordered someone, and the noise died down.

The bullet was now produced again and handed to the pathologist.

'Now, Dr. Menzies,' said Sir Benjamin. 'I should like to ask you about this bullet. You examined it as part of the evidence, did you not?'

'I did,' said Menzies.

'I understand that you have made something of a study of ballistics in recent years,' said Sir Benjamin, 'and have published a number of papers on the subject, with particular reference to the characteristics of bullets which have already been fired from a gun.'

'That is so.'

'Thank you. You will remember that some few weeks ago you were asked to examine the bullet you have in your hand. Let the record state that the bullet in question is the one which was extracted from the wall in the prisoner's flat. You will also remember that at the same time you were asked to examine a second bullet. Where was the second bullet from?'

'The second bullet was one I took from the body of a man in October last. He had been shot dead—I understand under perfectly justifiable circumstances—and I was brought in by the Home Office to examine his body.'

The second bullet was now produced and a bland Home Office functionary brought forth, who stated flatly, as though he were reading out the racing results, that this particular bullet came from a gun owned and fired by Mrs. Angela Marchmont, and that the matter had been looked into and she had been proved perfectly blameless—not to say praiseworthy, for the man she had shot was a dangerous criminal who had just attacked a woman. Here, there was a stir on the part of the public, who had, of course, read the story in the newspapers at the time. They were sternly instructed to hush, and Dr. Menzies was called to continue with his evidence, under the questioning of Sir Benjamin, who said:

'Please tell the court what it was you were looking for with respect to the two bullets.'

'I was asked whether it were possible to ascertain whether the bullet retrieved last October and the one which I understand was found in the prisoner's flat had been fired from the same gun,' said Dr. Menzies.

'And is it possible? Can such a thing be stated with certainty?'

'That depends on a number of factors—in particular the state of the bullets; however, in some circumstances yes, it is possible to state with reasonable certainty that two bullets were fired by the same weapon. The grooves inside the barrel of a gun often have their own individual characteristics caused by tiny, almost imperceptible defects, which may then cause scratches on a projectile as it passes down the barrel. These scratches are invisible to the naked eye, but if we examine the bullet under a microscope, they can be clearly seen.'

'And what can you tell us about the two bullets?'

Dr. Menzies then began a long explanation about lands and grooves, faults, erosions and patches of rust, which became somewhat technical. After several minutes of this Sir Benjamin, seeing that some members of the jury were beginning to develop a glazed look, and sensing that he was losing his audience, took the first opportunity to interject.

'And what was your conclusion?' he said.

'I was coming to that,' said Menzies. 'When I examined the two bullets side by side under a microscope, I noticed a highly distinctive, broad scratch on both of them—almost a notch—caused by a fault at the muzzle end of the gun. The two scratches were identical in every way. It was impossible to mistake it. This, together with one or two other suggestive but slightly less conclusive similarities, led me to believe that the two bullets were, in fact, fired from the same weapon.'

'Are you quite certain of that?' said Sir Benjamin.

'To the extent that one can be certain of anything, yes,' said Menzies.

'So then, for the benefit of the ladies and gentlemen of the jury, and just so we are quite clear on the matter, you believe that the bullet which was found in Mrs. Marchmont's flat was fired from the same gun that killed the man whose body you examined last October. That is, a revolver which is known to have been owned by Mrs. Marchmont herself?'

'That is so,' said Menzies, bowing his head.

Sir Benjamin paused a moment to let this sink in, although there was no need, for everybody had understood it perfectly well. On the press bench, Freddy and Kathie looked at one another in some dismay. The absence of any weapon in Angela's flat was a fact that might have been used by both the prosecution and the defence to support their respective cases, but now it was known for certain that it was Angela's gun, and not some other weapon, which had been used to kill Davie Marchmont, it looked all the worse for her. Mr. Travers for the defence would most likely have to reconsider his approach, for he could no longer suggest that some unknown person had killed Davie using a different weapon. Now he would have to explain how the killer had known where to find Angela's gun—and that would be difficult indeed.

The Attorney-General had not finished with Menzies, however. It appeared the great pathologist had also been given an article of clothing to look at and pronounce judgment upon. It was Mrs. Marchmont's black evening-dress—the one she had been wearing on the night of her husband's death. On examining the dress, Dr. Menzies had found a large stain near the hem, which further analysis had revealed to be blood.

'What did you deduce from that?' asked Sir Benjamin.

'Merely that whoever was wearing the dress had been in proximity to the deceased when he died or at some time soon after his death,' said Menzies.

Sir Benjamin had no further questions, and Mr. Travers now rose to cross-examine.

'Did you find any other patches of blood apart from that one near the hem?' he said.

'I did not,' said Dr. Menzies.

'Would you have expected to find other traces of blood on it, supposing the woman it belonged to had shot a man dead while wearing it?'

'I certainly might,' conceded Menzies. 'It would depend on a number of factors, but there might have been other traces of blood on the top half of the dress.'

'The patch of blood you found—it could not have been caused by the impact of the bullet as it entered?'

'No,' said Menzies. 'Quite apart from the fact that it was on the hem and thus near the bottom of the dress, the stain is quite inconsistent with the type of bloodstain which would be caused in the circumstances you describe. In the latter case, the bloodstain would take the form of a splatter of droplets, rather than a solid patch.'

Mr. Travers thanked him and Dr. Menzies stepped down. Inspector Scott was now recalled.

'Was the prisoner wearing the evening-dress we have just seen when you arrived at her flat?' said Sir Benjamin.

'No,' replied Scott. 'She was in ordinary day clothes.'

'I see,' said Sir Benjamin. 'Now, you have told me that Mrs. Marchmont said she did not discover her husband's body until about seven o'clock on the Sunday morning, and that she hardly went near the body. Did she have an explanation for the blood-stain on the evening dress? For it seems to imply that she did, in fact, approach her husband's body, and that she did so on the Saturday night.'

'She did, sir. She said that she had returned home after midnight feeling very tired, having drunk rather more than she was accustomed to, and so had got into bed and fallen asleep still wearing her evening-gown. The next morning, when she found Mr. Marchmont's body, she knelt down by him briefly with the intention of looking for a pulse, but then changed her mind. She then changed into normal day things before calling us.'

'Thank you,' said Sir Benjamin. 'Now, let us pass to the evidence of the gun—or rather the absence of the gun, for it appears to be missing. Where was the gun kept?'

'The prisoner told us it was always kept in the second drawer of a chest by the window.'

'And we know it was not found there, or anywhere else in the flat. Was the chest of drawers tested for finger-prints?'

'Yes, it was, and there were none except for those of Mrs. Marchmont, which we found on the handles of both the second drawer and the top drawer.'

'That indicates that Mrs. Marchmont was the last person to open those drawers, yes?'

'Yes.'

'Has a search been made for the gun?'

'As far as possible, but London is a big place and there was ample opportunity between the time of Mr. Marchmont's death and the time we arrived for someone to have disposed of it,' said Inspector Scott. 'It is quite possible that it will never be found.'

Mr. Travers began his cross-examination.

'Had there been any attempt made to hide or destroy the evening-dress?' he said.

'No,' said Scott. 'It was thrown on a chair in the bedroom.'

'If the prisoner had disposed of the gun in a calculated manner, as has been suggested by my learned friend, might not one have expected her also to dispose of the dress at the same time?'

'Not if she hadn't realized there was a bloodstain on it,' said Scott.

Mr. Travers nodded.

'Now, then, as to the finger-prints on the chest of drawers. It's rather odd, don't you think, that the prisoner's were the only ones found on it, and that it was otherwise clean? Mrs. Marchmont has a maid. Surely one would have expected there to be more than one set of prints on the chest—especially since the maid was away at the time.'

Inspector Scott conceded that it was unusual to find so few finger-prints on an item of furniture of this kind, but suggested that perhaps the prisoner had cleaned it herself.

'And then put more finger-prints on it?' said Mr. Travers. 'I put it to you that Mrs. Marchmont might easily have touched the chest of drawers for quite an innocent reason when she came home that evening, but that there is no reason at all for her prints to have been the only ones on the chest unless it had been deliberately wiped clean before she touched it.'

'It is possible, I suppose,' said Scott politely, although he was clearly not convinced by the argument.

The defence had no further questions, and Inspector Scott stood down.

The prosecution then set itself to looking at the alibi evidence, and called one William Tibbs, the prisoner's chauffeur, who testified, pink in the face and looking deeply uncomfortable all the while, that he had driven his employer to a ball at Lord Wymington's house in Lowndes Square at nine o'clock on the evening in question. Mrs. Marchmont had then sent him away, saying that he need not wait, as she did not know when she would be coming home. He had seen nothing more of her until the next day, by which time the police were already at the flat. At this point he glanced over to the prisoner, who gave him an encouraging smile, whereupon he went even pinker than before, and then he was dismissed.

He was followed by Mr. Alfred Pearson, who stated that he had been playing cards at Burkett's club in company with David Marchmont and one or two other men on the evening in question, and that as far as he could remember, the deceased had left the club at about nine o'clock. No, he had not said where he was going.

The last witness for the day was Mrs. Edrys Lawrence, whose name most people present recognized from the society pages. She threw a look at Angela which was intended to be rueful and deeply sympathetic, but which emerged as a simper, and then testified, with a tendency to digression, that she had been at a charity ball with Mrs. Marchmont on the night in question, and that Angela had come to her at midnight to say that she did not feel well and would go home.

'Are you certain it was midnight?' said Sir Benjamin.

'Oh, yes,' said Mrs. Lawrence earnestly. 'I remember it particularly because everybody had already started smashing the rabbit.'

There was a puzzled pause, as perhaps nine-tenths of those present in court wondered whether this was some sort of new upper-class slang, referring to who knew what manner of debauchery, and then the Attorney-General invited her to explain. She did so in some confusion, at which those in the public gallery shook their heads at the odd things high society got up to. She was then excused, Sir Benjamin took one last glance at himself in the reflective surface of a nearby brass paper-weight, and proceedings adjourned for the day.

CHAPTER FIFTEEN

THE NEXT DAY the prosecution continued in its efforts to demonstrate that Davie Marchmont must have been killed after midnight on the eleventh of November, and produced Mrs. Theodora Trumpington, who gave her address as Flat 10, 23 Mount Street, Mayfair. She was a stout, elderly woman with a red face, a tweed suit and a quantity of wiry grey hair which showed signs of wanting to escape from its moorings, for every so often another lock would work its way out from under her hat and stand to attention. She glared round at the court and then peered suspiciously at the Attorney-General as though he were about to ask her for money. Sir Benjamin produced his most winning smile.

'Mrs. Trumpington, you live in the flat next door to the prisoner, I believe,' he began.

'You know very well I do,' she said. 'I told them so before I got here.'

'Indeed you did,' he said smoothly, 'and I know you will not mind repeating it for the benefit of the court. Are you acquainted with Mrs. Marchmont at all?'

'I've seen her, of course,' said Mrs. Trumpington. 'Very polite young woman. Always says good morning and smiles. Doesn't wipe her feet on the mat before she goes in, though. I tell her that dirty shoes will ruin her parquet but she never listens, and now look what's happened.'

Here she turned to Angela and wagged a finger.

'I told you,' she said, then turned back to Sir Benjamin with the look of someone who had been proved right in her sad predictions.

Ignoring the implication that Angela's muddy shoes had led directly to the death of Angela's husband and her trial for his murder, Sir Benjamin went on:

'You were at home on the night of Saturday the tenth of November last?'

'Yes, of course,' she said. 'Where else should I have been?'

'I don't know,' said Sir Benjamin politely. 'Now, I should like you to think back to that night if you can. Do you remember hearing any noise at all? Can you hear people entering and leaving the building, for example?'

'Not as a rule,' said Mrs. Trumpington. 'The walls are rather thick. It's a solidly-built place. That's why I like it. I can't bear it when the walls are so thin that one can hear one's neighbours chewing their food next door.'

'Then you heard no-one arrive that night?'

'No.'

'Was there any other noise?'

'Yes, there most certainly was,' she exclaimed suddenly. 'Banging and crashing and whizzing all night, they were.'

'Who were?'

'Why, the fireworks, of course. They ought to be banned. They're nothing but a nuisance.'

'Ah, you say that people were letting off fireworks outside,' said Sir Benjamin. 'Yes, it is a frequent occurrence at that time of year. When you say "all night," do you mean that there were many such explosions that night?'

'Oh, dozens,' said Mrs. Trumpington.

'Are you quite sure of that?' said Sir Benjamin gently. 'Dozens would indeed be many, and I shouldn't blame you at all for being upset at the disturbance if that were the case. But I should like you to think carefully about the number, if you would. This is a court proceeding and a woman's life is at stake, and I am sure you would not wish to see justice badly served.'

'Of course not,' said Mrs. Trumpington gruffly. She shuffled slightly and half-glanced at Angela, and another lock of hair fell out of her hat. 'Well, then, perhaps not dozens,' she admitted.

'A dozen?'

She thought.

'I should say six or seven,' she said at last.

'And can you remember at what time you heard them?'

'Mostly after I was in bed,' she said. 'That's what made me so cross. I sleep badly in the early part of the night, as a rule, and I require absolute quiet to drop off.'

'At what time did you go to bed?'

'Somewhere between half past ten and a quarter to eleven,' she said. 'I go at about the same time every night.'

'But you could not get to sleep because of the bangs? Can you remember at what time you heard the first one?'

'At twenty to one,' she said.

'Can you be sure of that?'

'Oh, yes,' she said. 'I'd just started to drift off when it happened, and I turned my lamp on and looked at the clock.'

'And did the other noises follow immediately afterwards?'

'No,' she said. 'They came all together a few minutes later.'

'And you were in no doubt that they were fireworks, and not gunshots?'

'Of course not,' she said. 'Guns don't go "whee—pfft!"'

Her imitation was an enthusiastic one, and the spectators giggled. Sir Benjamin smiled appreciatively.

'Did they all make that noise?' he said. 'Even the first one?'

'Well, no—as I said, the first one went bang,' said Mrs. Trumpington.

'Then presumably that one might have been a gunshot.'

'I suppose it might,' she said, after a moment's thought. 'Although it didn't strike me as such at the time.'

This was quite sufficient for Sir Benjamin's purposes, however, and he invited the defence to cross-examine. Mr. Travers stood.

'You said that the noises you heard came *mostly* after you were in bed,' he said. 'Does that mean you heard others before you went to bed?'

'Only one,' said Mrs. Trumpington. 'That was the loudest one of all, but at least it didn't come when I was trying to get to sleep.'

'What time was it?'

'Just after ten, I should say.'

'And it was very loud?'

'Oh, tremendously,' she said.

'And was that one a bang or a—er—whizz?' said Mr. Travers.

'It was a bang. Most definitely a bang,' she said firmly. 'I almost jumped out of my skin when I heard it. In fact, for a second I thought someone had let the thing off inside the building, and I was worried about fire.'

'Might *that* one have been a gunshot, do you suppose?' said Mr. Travers.

She agreed that it might. There were no further questions, and she was allowed to stand down, which she did, with one last glare round at the court.

Having dealt with the matter of the alibi to its satisfaction, the prosecution then turned its attention to the question of motive. Inspector Scott was recalled once again, and was asked whether Mrs. Marchmont had had an explanation as to why her husband had come all the way from New York to find her, if they were separated. Here the spectators sat up and prepared to pay close attention, for this looked like being the most interesting part of the trial.

Inspector Scott recounted what Angela had told him about her husband's request for money. There then followed the evidence of the cheque-book, and there was a gasp from the public gallery as it was revealed that Mrs. Marchmont had written her husband a cheque for five hundred pounds with apparently no more concern than if she were paying the milkman. This was a sum indeed, and the public spectators now eyed the prisoner with respect and envy, and not a little suspicion. They knew, of course, that those in high society were quite accustomed to bandy about large amounts of cash and think nothing of it, but this was something quite different. Not the least odd was the fact that *she* had given *him* the money, rather than the other way about. What business had a husband to be sponging on his wife when he ought to be supporting her instead? Anyone looking at the public gallery at that moment might have observed a number of heads wagging as the spectators jumped to various conclusions—one of which was that the dead man must have had some kind of hold over his wife.

'Did she say why she gave him such an enormous sum?' inquired Sir Benjamin, who had himself only the day before made out a cheque for a similar amount of money to a young lady whom he maintained discreetly in a flat in Chelsea, and who relied upon him to defray her day-to-day expenses.

'She said she gave him it because he asked for it, and he was still her husband, after all,' replied Scott.

There was some muttering among the women on the public bench about this, much of which was to the effect that had it been *their* husband coming to beg that sort of money, he might have whistled for it.

Inspector Scott made way then for a man from the bank, who stated that Mr. David Marchmont had come into his bank on Thursday the eighth of November and presented a cheque, drawn on the account of Mrs. Angela Marchmont, in return for which—after the usual formalities—he had received a cash sum of five hundred pounds.

'Was Mrs. Marchmont easily able to afford such a sum?' said Sir Benjamin.

'I shouldn't say *easily*,' said the man from the bank. 'Mrs. Marchmont's financial position is an extremely healthy one, but much of her wealth is tied up in stocks, bonds and other securities. The five hundred pounds drawn left her with less than a hundred pounds in her current account.'

'But presumably she could have sold some of her investments if she had needed any more money?'

'That is correct,' said the man from the bank.

'Thank you,' said Sir Benjamin.

Alfred Pearson was now recalled, and repeated what he had already told Freddy about Davie Marchmont's behaviour at Burkett's on the night of his death; how he had carelessly thrown down large sums of money at cards, and how he had claimed that there was plenty more where that came from.

'What did you understand him to mean by that?' asked Sir Benjamin.

'Why, I don't know,' said Pearson. 'I suppose I thought he had been put on to a good thing by someone—perhaps a horse, or an investment.'

'He said nothing about asking his wife for more money?'

'No. As a matter of fact, I had no idea he was married until I heard he was dead.'

Mr. Pearson was thanked and allowed to go, and the indefatigable Inspector Scott called once more.

'I understand the prisoner and the deceased were married in New York and lived there together for some years,' said Sir Benjamin. 'Did you, as part of your investigation, communicate with the police in that city?'

'Yes, we did,' said Scott.

'And what did they tell you?'

Inspector Scott cleared his throat.

'Since Mr. and Mrs. Marchmont had separated shortly before Mrs. Marchmont returned to England, we wished to find out whether there was known to have been any trouble between the deceased and his wife while they were living together in New York,' he said. 'They informed us that they had, on one occasion in early nineteen twenty-six, been called out to an address on Fifth Avenue, as there were reports of an altercation. When the police arrived at the apartment, they spoke to Mr. David Marchmont, who claimed that it had all been a misunderstanding. Mrs. Angela Marchmont was also present, and refused to say anything, and so the police went away. The next day, they received a call from the mother of Mr. Marchmont, accusing Mrs. Marchmont of having threatened her husband with a gun and demanding that they arrest her, but since neither of the people directly involved wished to press charges, no further action was taken.'

'It was in nineteen twenty-six that the Marchmonts separated and Mrs. Marchmont returned to England, yes?' said Sir Benjamin.

'So I understand,' said Inspector Scott.

'And she had not seen him since then?'

'That is what she said,' replied Scott.

The inspector was excused and the court adjourned for lunch. Outside the building, Freddy and Kathie were joined by Inspector Alec Jameson, who had managed to take a little time from his duties to run over from Scotland Yard and find out how things were getting along. His wife threw herself into his arms and shook her head at his inquiring expression.

'It's not going well, I take it,' he said.

'Not exactly,' said Freddy. 'Of course, it's the prosecution's day, so things are bound to look bad, but I must say they're doing the devil of a job in building up a case against her. It doesn't help that she apparently used to amuse herself by waving a gun at him once in a while when they lived in New York.'

'She didn't!' said Jameson.

'We don't know that,' said Kathie. 'No charges were ever brought. It might not be true.'

'I don't know,' said Freddy. 'From what I've heard of this chap he sounds as though he was something of a blister. I should imagine even you'd have wanted to wave a gun at him, Kathie—especially if you'd been forced to live with the fellow for years while he took all your money and paraded his women before you.'

'Oh, he was one of those types, was he?' said Jameson. 'Poor Angela.'

'Yes,' said Freddy. 'And the worst of it is, none of that has come out in court yet. When it does it won't make the deceased look good, but old Ben won't care about that. His concern is to give Angela a motive, and I have the feeling he's planning to give her both barrels this afternoon.'

'Why do you say that?' said Jameson.

'Because I understand they've shipped over the dead man's mother, who's simply dying to have her say,' said Freddy. 'And I don't think she's going to be recommending Angela for a medal.'

CHAPTER SIXTEEN

DELLA MARCHMONT DELANEY was a woman whom it was unwise to cross. For many years her acid tongue and bare-faced put-downs had made her the scourge of New York society, and nobody would have supposed from the grand house she lived in, the evening parties she attended and the appearances she maintained, that she had barely two pennies to rub together. Twice a widow, she had lived for her only son and child, who was the apple of her eye and could do no wrong even while doing wrong. With such a mother it was a brave woman indeed who would dare marry him, and Della had disliked and mistrusted Angela from the start, for she did not understand this self-possessed young Englishwoman who had come to America and worked her way into the confidence of Della's brother-in-law, Carey Bernstein, so easily. What business did a woman have in running a company? Especially when there was a perfectly good nephew in the form of Davie to be groomed in the management of the Bernstein empire.

It did not occur to Della that Bernstein had the measure of his nephew and had no intention of allowing Davie anywhere near his business if he could help it, for he could see perfectly well what sort of fist Davie would make of it. The cool-headed Angela had just the right sort of brain for the job, on the other hand, even if she was a woman, and she very soon proved herself to be quite up to the responsibility of running Bernstein & Associates. Della, of course, did not see it in this light, and had the worst sort of suspicions about how Angela had managed to attain such a position of trust—suspicions which were completely unfounded, but nonetheless deeply rooted.

When Bernstein died suddenly, leaving a half share in Bernstein & Associates to Angela (at least he had had the decency to leave *something* to his only nephew), Della was exceedingly put out—and even more so when her darling son announced only a few months later that he and Angela were going to get married. Della did her best to dissuade him, but Davie had always been one to do as he pleased, and he merely laughed at her. So the wedding went ahead, and Della found some comfort in the thought that at least Angela brought with her the other half of the company which ought rightfully to belong wholly to her son. After their marriage, Angela would, of course, step down and leave the running of the firm to Davie, while she went about providing Della with some grandchildren to play off against one another. But months and years went by and nothing of the sort happened. Angela kept her position at the head of Bernstein & Associates and Davie continued his life of idleness, and no children appeared. Della grew increasingly impatient at this state of affairs and one day decided to confront her son, who replied carelessly that there would be no children, and that he had no intention of forcing Angela to give up work, for he was quite happy as he was. Della seethed with rage at this, but did not argue with Davie, for she knew it would be useless. Still, she observed them as closely as she could, for she hoped that one day her son might be persuaded to give the marriage up. She knew he had other women, and that he appeared to be living in a state of ease and dissipation, but supposed that Angela was either unaware of the fact or did not care, for she had become increasingly withdrawn and silent, and was seen less and less in the company of her husband. Naturally, Della assumed that Angela's apparent coldness was the reason for Davie's association with other women, and had no idea that it was in fact caused by it, or that Angela was by now very unhappy.

So things continued until one day Davie happened to mention, quite in passing, that Angela had bought out his share of Bernstein & Associates some years earlier, and that he was entirely reliant upon her for money. Della was horrified and urged him to divorce Angela, for it was by now clear that they were no longer living as man and wife, and the thought of her son having to beg from that woman was more than she could bear. Even poverty would be better than this, she said. What if Angela decided to stop supporting him? But Davie laughed and said he was quite happy as he was, for he could live as he chose and was assured of money whenever he wanted it. His wife would never say no—not if she wanted to keep her reputation, at any rate, for he knew things about her which she would never wish to be made public. And then he told Della all about

Angela and why she would never divorce him, however much she wanted to, and why he would never have to work again.

It was shortly after this that the police were called to the Marchmonts' apartment after it was reported that Mrs. Marchmont had threatened her husband with a gun. A week later Angela packed her bags and returned to England, and they had not seen her again. Two and a half years after that, Davie had gone to London after his wife, never to return. Della had always known that nothing good would come of his marriage to the upstart Englishwoman, and now she had been proved right. She had lost her darling, and today she wanted revenge.

As the name 'Della Marchmont Delaney' was pronounced, the court sat up, abuzz with interest, for it seemed as though the real excitement were about to begin. Mrs. Delaney made her way with great deliberation to the witness-box and gave her oath in a clipped American accent, and as she did so all those present feasted their eyes upon her. Although she must have been approaching seventy, she was evidently not one to lie down and allow the years to trample over her, for every inch of her spoke of a relentless battle against the forces of time. Her hair was an exquisite shade of gold, and gleamed defiantly under the lights. Her hooded eyes were heavy with black, her cheeks a delicate pink. Her attire was splendid, fashionable and fitted to a nicety. Only her hands betrayed her real age, for they were clawed, grasping and bony, but she did her best to hide them under bracelets and rings that jangled and clinked as she moved.

She stood and waited, looking straight ahead, as Sir Benjamin prepared to begin. Not once did she look at Angela, who knew what was coming and was bracing herself. The Attorney-General knew he had a strong case, but he also knew that Mrs. Delaney had a spite against her daughter-in-law which might prejudice the jury against her. Still, she had important evidence to give, and for that reason he was determined to handle her carefully—not least because she must not be allowed to realize that his purpose in questioning her was to establish beyond all doubt a motive for the crime. *She* believed that she had come to turn the court against Angela, but what Sir Benjamin really wanted was to reveal Davie Marchmont's true character and to show just what sort of man it was who might drive a woman to murder.

'You are the mother of David Marchmont, yes?' he said.

'I am,' she replied.

'You live in New York, I understand.'

She replied in the affirmative.

'Did you live with your son?'

'No. He had his own place, which he shared with his wife until they separated, and I had mine.'

'At whose instigation did the separation occur?'

'At hers,' said Della.

'Do you know why she left?'

'He said it was because they didn't get along any more,' she replied shortly.

'Only that they didn't get along?' said Sir Benjamin. 'Are you quite sure that was all there was to it?'

'What do you mean?' said Della.

'Why, that women do not generally just leave their husbands on such a slight motive. I beg your pardon, but are you sure that there was no indiscretion on his part, for example?'

Della did not answer immediately. She seemed to be delib-
erating.

'Davie was a good-looking man,' she said at last. 'Women
liked him and you could hardly blame him if he liked them
back. But they were no more than passing amusements. Men
do it, and a good wife forgives. I guess your wife forgives *you*,
doesn't she?'

As it happened, Lady Hicks-Reddington was quite unaware
of the existence of the young lady in Chelsea—or so Sir Benjamin hoped. He was much too sure of himself to be even
slightly discomposed by Della's remark, however, and since
his questioning had achieved the desired result, which was to
expose Davie Marchmont as the adulterer he had been, he now
moved on to a different subject.

'Do you remember when it was that you last saw your son?'
he said.

'It was in late October last year. We had lunch together, as
we did frequently.'

'Did he tell you he was planning to come to England to see
his wife?'

'No,' said Mrs. Delaney. 'I had no idea of it. If I had, I'd have
tried to talk him out of it.'

'Why is that?'

'Because no good could have come of it.'

'Can you explain why you believe that?' said Sir Benjamin.

Mrs. Delaney paused and weighed her words. Sir Benjamin
need not have worried that she would ruin his case, for she was
perfectly aware of the need to appear measured and moderate
in her evidence.

'I didn't want Angela to turn against him even more than she already had,' she said eventually.

'What do you suppose was his purpose in coming to England? To effect a reconciliation with his wife, perhaps?'

'No. Of course not. It was too late for that.'

'Some other purpose, then.'

'I imagine he needed money,' she said reluctantly.

'Oh?' said Sir Benjamin. 'And he intended to ask Mrs. Marchmont for it? Was he accustomed to receive money from her?'

'He had no choice,' she said, and her hooded eyes gleamed angrily. 'He had nothing of his own and relied totally on her for support.'

'Your son did not work in New York, then?'

'He was in business when he first married,' she said. 'His wife had a share in the company too, but after a few years she bought him out and left him with nothing to do. After that he felt useless and couldn't settle to anything else.'

'Why did he feel useless?'

'It's not right for a man to do nothing while his wife goes out to work. She made him feel worthless. He had to come to her whenever he needed money.'

'But you said Mrs. Marchmont bought his share of the company. Surely that must have provided him with a lump sum to live off?'

Mrs. Delaney hesitated.

'He was never especially good at looking after money,' she said at length. 'He had a little trouble holding on to it.'

Sir Benjamin paused for a moment, while the words 'idle good-for-nothing' ran through the minds of the majority of those present, just as he had intended they should.

'Did Mrs. Marchmont ever refuse to give him the money he asked for?' he said at length.

'I don't believe so,' replied Mrs. Delaney.

'Then she was generous to her husband, even though they were no longer living together?'

'I wouldn't call it generous. He had to keep coming back for more. And when she left for England the funds dried up.'

'Did she want to divorce him?'

'Maybe she did. I don't know. I thought myself they'd be better off apart, but Davie said he couldn't afford to live without her. He was trapped, he said, and the only guarantee he had that she wouldn't divorce him was the fact that he knew something that she didn't want put about, and could speak at any time.'

'He was blackmailing her, you mean?'

Della hesitated as she realized how she had sounded.

'That's an ugly word,' she said. 'Of course it wasn't blackmail. They had an agreement, he told me. It was quite above the board. She would keep him in funds and he would make sure that nobody found out about it.'

'Found out about what?' said Sir Benjamin, and his voice was as smooth as silk.

Della licked her lips. She had come a long way to spite her daughter-in-law. It was all she could do not to turn her head and look at Angela.

'About the child,' she said.

There was a momentary stir in court, then silence. Freddy and Kathie looked blankly at one other.

'Which child?' said Sir Benjamin.

'Why, Angela's,' said Mrs. Delaney, and the spite dripped from her tone as her anger grew. 'That's what she brought to the marriage: a bastard child. My son took her on out of the kindness of his heart when nobody else would have touched her, and this is the thanks he got.'

At this sensation everybody started talking at once, and there was some ado to quiet the court. The only person who seemed unaffected by the revelation was Angela, who continued to look straight ahead. Outwardly nobody could have told what she was thinking, for she seemed as calm as ever, but inside she was in turmoil. She had known, of course, that this was coming, and had done her best to steel herself against it, but it was still a blow to the heart to hear it stated so baldly in front of so many people, by someone who wished her nothing but ill. Still, the worst was over now, she thought, and she had nothing left to hear that could hurt her. In this, she was wrong, as it happened, but for the present she felt a little relief, at least.

Sir Benjamin was congratulating himself on having drawn Della out so effectively, but hid it well.

'The child was not Mr. Marchmont's, then?' he said, when the noise had died down.

'No,' said Della. 'The story was that she was engaged to someone else before she married Davie, but he died. I don't know whether that's true, but she was caught out, all right.'

'And what became of the child?'

'She was sent to England to live with some relation or other when she was very young,' said Della. 'Barbara, I think her name is. I don't know where she is now. The whole thing was kept secret. I didn't know about it myself until Davie told me long afterwards.'

'Mr. Marchmont did not adopt her?'

'No,' said Della. 'What would he want with someone else's child?'

'And yet you say he married Mrs. Marchmont out of the kindness of his heart. Presumably that kindness did not extend to accepting his wife's daughter as his own.'

'The child was quite well where it was,' said Mrs. Delaney. 'That's what Davie told me. And what use would there have been in bringing her over to live with them? Angela had no time for her. She would only have been in the way.'

'Let me see if I have understood this correctly,' said Sir Benjamin. 'Your son married Angela Marchmont in the full knowledge that she had an illegitimate daughter, but rather than adopt the child as his own, he instead demanded money from his wife in return for his silence on the matter. In fact, he went so far as to follow her to England and hound her for even more money after the marriage had irretrievably failed and she might justifiably have thought herself rid of him.'

Under her face-powder, Mrs. Delaney flushed angrily.

'That's not how it was at all,' she snapped. 'He was penniless, and it was the only way he could persuade Angela to help him. There was no question of blackmail. I won't have you saying things like that about my son. Davie was a good man at heart, and his only mistake was in marrying *her*.'

Here she nodded over her shoulder at Angela. Sir Benjamin glanced at his reflection in the paper-weight and was satisfied. Things had gone better than he had expected. Della Marchmont Delaney had been the perfect witness for his purposes, and had left the court in no doubt that Davie Marchmont had been the worst sort of cad and that Angela Marchmont had had every reason to take a gun and shoot him dead.

CHAPTER SEVENTEEN

THAT CONCLUDED THE case for the prosecution, and even Mr. Travers had to admit that Sir Benjamin had played his hand well. There were one or two holes in the prosecution's story, he said to Angela, and it would be Mr. Travers' task to enlarge those holes bit by bit until the jury was in so much doubt that it would have no choice but to acquit—but still, there was no denying that it would be an uphill battle.

'It is unfortunate,' he said, 'that this story of your daughter had to come out, for of course it appears to give you a very strong motive. However, forewarned is forearmed, as they say, and we must do what we can with it. Where is Barbara now, by the way? I seem to remember you told me she lives mostly with relations of her father.'

'Yes,' said Angela. 'They're in India at the moment, and she's been taken out of school and sent there to join them for a few weeks until this is all over. I didn't want her to have to face ridicule from her class-mates when it all came out. Not that

I think she'd put up with that sort of thing for an instant, but still, I thought it was best.'

In fact, she was by no means certain that this was the case, for she knew Barbara was not the kind of girl to suffer being sent out of the way while such a thing was going on. As the trial went on, Angela had every moment expected to hear that Barbara had run off and was heading back to England, and she lived in fear that she would one day see the girl sitting in the public gallery, glaring at Angela in righteous outrage at having been kept out of things. Barbara had always believed she was an orphan, and Angela had no idea how she would take the news that the woman she had always thought of as her godmother was in fact her mother, but the thought of how hurt Barbara might feel did nothing at all to assuage Angela's feelings of guilt. It would surely be hard on her, though, to find out that her mother was alive and well, only to see her hanged weeks afterwards for murder—for by now Angela was quite certain that her trial could have only one outcome.

Odd as it seemed, Angela had spent so many years regretting her ill-advised marriage to Davie Marchmont that by now she barely gave it any thought. For herself, it was nothing—she had learnt to live with her mistake, and for the most part had done very well in spite of him. But Barbara was a different matter, since she had suffered unknowingly as a consequence of it all. Davie had known about Angela's engagement to Jack Wells, and how the proud young Englishman had died in a tragic motor accident only ten days before their wedding; had guessed, too, about Angela's additional source of grief, and why Carey Bernstein had allowed her to absent herself from her duties for some weeks only a few months afterwards. She had then gone to Europe with Bernstein on business while the war was at its height, and had returned some time later, still pale and sad. Davie encouraged her to confide in him, and at length she did, and soon after that they were engaged and then married. He seemed understanding about Angela's position, and implied that he would adopt Barbara as his own, but it swiftly became clear that he intended to do no such thing. Instead, he had used his wife's secret as a weapon against her almost from the start. In such a situation, Angela could not bring herself to send to England for her daughter, who had been staying with Jack's sister and her husband, for how could it benefit the girl to grow up surrounded by such unhappiness? No, she was much better off where she was.

After Angela returned to England it seemed she and Barbara were doomed to remain nothing more than friendly acquaintances, for the sad fact was that Angela had not the first idea about motherhood after so many childless years, whereas Nina and Gerald had a brood of their own and were quite happy to include Barbara in it, and give her the family life she could not have enjoyed with Angela and Davie. Moreover, there was still no getting around the fact of Barbara's illegitimacy, which was a heavy burden to lay upon a child, and so all in all it seemed safest to maintain the fiction that she was an orphan. Angela had always meant to tell Barbara the truth one day, but had continually put off the decision to do so until it had become too difficult. Now the secret had come to light in the most public way possible, and in addition to all her other woes Angela was now racked with guilt at the thought of the effect the trial would have on her daughter—although she was beginning to think Barbara would be much better off without her, for there was no denying that she seemed to have made rather a mess of things.

Involuntarily, her thoughts turned to Edgar Valencourt, and she wondered where he was and what he was doing. Had he read in the newspapers about her arrest and trial? If he had indeed gone to France as he had said, then it was quite likely that he knew nothing about what was going on at present; at least, she hoped that were the case, for it was too painful to her to think that he might be perfectly aware of her plight and observing it helplessly—or even indifferently—from afar. Perhaps he had reached South America already and was busy establishing a new life for himself. If so, then he would certainly know nothing, and by the time he found out what had happened she would probably be long dead. Still, she stood firm in her belief that naming him would do nothing to help her cause—and in fact would be more likely to harm it. Her reputation was already battered enough, but some pride still remained to her and she did not wish to damage it any further by having all her sins put on public display at once. If some miracle occurred and she were acquitted, there would be enough work in trying to live down what had already been revealed. Angela wondered which, if any, of her friends would prove loyal in that event. Her brother Humphrey was doing his best; he had sent her a stiff letter of support, even though she knew that the very idea of such a thing happening in the family must horrify him. Other friends had sent messages of varying degrees of sincerity. Freddy she was certain of, but there was no saying how some of her more distant acquaintances might regard her now that they knew the truth.

At that, Angela remembered William and Marthe, those two most faithful of servants. Poor William had evidently been upset at being called to appear for the prosecution, although he had had nothing to tell that could harm her. Marthe could be trusted to keep quiet about Valencourt—and in any case there was no reason why she should suppose that he might have had anything to do with Davie's death at all, for she had seen him only briefly a few days before the murder. She and William had proved themselves wholly trustworthy and for that she silently thanked them, but still, they would soon need to find new situations when the inevitable happened. Perhaps it would be better if she released them from her service immediately, in fact. She would, of course, write them excellent references—although she had no idea how a new employer might look upon the word of a convicted murderess. She hoped her reputation would not harm their prospects. Yes, perhaps she would give them notice now. They were welcome to remain until they had found something that suited, naturally, but the least she could do was to allow them plenty of time to make the necessary arrangements.

Having reached this decision, Angela wrote the letters and the references immediately, for she felt that there was no time to lose. They would be sent out later, and Marthe and William would be free, and then she would have one less thing to worry about. After she had finished, she sat, thinking of what was to come. The case for the defence was due to begin the next day, and all she could do now was trust that Mr. Travers, with Freddy's help, would somehow produce some evidence that would exonerate her. It was a small hope, but at present it was the only one she had.

CHAPTER EIGHTEEN

THE CASE FOR the defence opened on Friday morning. The crowd outside the Old Bailey had swelled to almost twice the size of the first day, for the whole country, it seemed, had been eagerly following the progress of the trial in the newspapers, and hundreds of people formed a queue down the street, agog to see what, if anything, the defence might have up its sleeve. The revelation about Angela Marchmont's love-child had been more sensational than any of the observers had expected even in their wildest imaginings, and the popular papers had lingered over the story with outward solemnity and inward glee. Now it remained to be seen what sort of weapon Angela might have in her armoury to defend herself against the charge of killing this husband of hers, who had clearly been a scoundrel of the worst sort. By now there was a fair amount of sympathy for her among the wider public, but the facts which could not but awaken their compassion were, of course, the very facts which gave her an undeniable motive for murder. The law was not concerned about whether the prisoner were worthy of sympathy or not—murder was murder, and justice must be pursued to the bitter end.

As the crowd filed in, Freddy and Kathie took their usual seats on the press bench.

'Now, this is Percy's opportunity to shine,' said Freddy. 'I've seen him in action before. He's not much to look at, and he's certainly not as showy as old Ben, but once he gets going he's rather impressive. I should like to see what he makes of the case.'

'Do you really think he can do anything?' said Kathie. 'The prosecution's argument seemed so conclusive.'

'I can't deny he did a good job,' admitted Freddy. 'That touch with the mother-in-law was particularly effective. There was no need at all to bring her over here, since there's plenty of physical evidence against Angela and motive proves nothing, but I suppose he wanted to end with a flourish of trumpets and dancing-girls. It was pure showing off, if you ask me.'

'Poor Angela,' said Kathie. 'And poor Barbara. I hope they've managed to keep the news from her. Do you know what Mr. Travers is planning to say?'

'Some of it,' said Freddy. 'We've found one or two witnesses who don't sound like much, but their evidence is suggestive, to say the least, and with a following wind he might be able to eke them out a bit. Remember, he doesn't have to prove her innocent. All he has to do is to plant enough doubt in the minds of the jury to make them uncertain whether she's guilty or not.'

'But surely the best way to do that would be to find out who really killed him?'

'Naturally,' said Freddy. 'But so far no-one has conveniently stepped forward and confessed to it, and I don't suppose they ever will.'

He was cross with himself, for he had been sure he would be able to find more witnesses, but even his search for the taxi driver had come up with nothing, and he had had no luck at all in tracing the foreign-looking man who had been seen arguing with Davie Marchmont on the steps of Burkett's. Now they must rely on very little, when what they really needed was some strong evidence to refute the prosecution's case and shake the conviction of the jury.

'It's such a pity the police fastened upon Angela so quickly as the only suspect,' said Kathie. 'I'm sure Inspector Scott is a very good detective, but he can't possibly have investigated the thing thoroughly enough. I only wish Alec could have taken the case, but we were away at the time. I wanted to go to Scotland, you see, because I'd never been. Perhaps we ought to have waited until the spring, and then this might never have happened.'

For a moment she looked stricken with guilt.

'Don't worry, old girl,' said Freddy. 'Nothing you could have done would have changed all this. Jameson wouldn't have been allowed to investigate it anyway, don't you see?'

'I suppose not,' said Kathie. 'Still, he might have given Inspector Scott a hint or two.'

Freddy opened his mouth to reply but was given no opportunity for just then there was a sudden bustle, and a voice instructed everyone to rise, and proceedings began for the day.

The first witness was Marthe Guillot, maid to the prisoner, who confirmed that she had left her keys with Madame on the day she left for France. No, she had not seen them since, and did not know what had become of them. They were certainly nowhere in the flat. Her evidence was brief and to the point, and she was allowed to step down, which she did after darting a glance at Angela.

The next person to take the stand was one Josiah McLeod, unemployed and of no fixed abode. Mr. Travers and Freddy had done their best with him; he had been cleaned up, given a shave and a new suit of clothes, and drilled in the art of speaking in public without mumbling, spitting or invoking the Deity. He had also been kept away from all sources of alcohol the day before he was due to testify, but by Friday morning his hands were trembling and his eyes watering, and so in the end it was judged better to give him a nip or two of whisky to steady him, with the promise of more after he had finished. The drink took immediate effect, and by the time he was nudged into the witness-box, he was tolerably firm on his feet.

Mr. Travers drew Jos out gently, and the spectators listened in fascination at the story he had to tell, which was simple enough. When he repeated what the second man had said to Davie Marchmont about shooting him as he would a dog, there was a collective sigh of satisfaction from the public gallery, for if anything had been wanting in the case up to now, it was a rival suspect. A man such as Davie Marchmont must have had enemies, for it was surely not possible that, with such a character, his wife was the only person he had ever offended. Now it looked as though here were another possible murderer—one, moreover, who had actually been overheard threatening to shoot the dead man. Of course, one did not like to take the word of a tramp, but this one was speaking soberly enough, and there was no reason to suppose he was lying.

'Might the threat to shoot Mr. Marchmont have been a joke?' inquired Mr. Travers.

'I don't reckon so,' said Jos. 'It sounded deadly serious to me. I shouldn't have liked to be in this dead chap's shoes meself and have had to hear it.'

'And what did Mr. Marchmont say to the threat?'

'He never said anything. The other feller walked away before he had the chance.'

'What did Mr. Marchmont do then?'

'Stood for a minute, a bit surprised, like. Then he picked something up off the ground and put it in his pocket and went off.'

'He picked something up? What was it?'

'Looked like a glove to me. Can't be sure, but it might've been, anyhow.'

'Was it his own glove?'

'I don't know. He already had gloves on, but he might have had a spare pair with him. Who knows how many pairs of fancy gloves these rich gents own?'

'Quite,' said Mr. Travers.

Sir Benjamin stepped up to cross-examine.

'Pardon me, Mr. McLeod, but am I right in supposing that you had been drinking on the day in question?'

Jos shuffled uncomfortably and admitted that that was the case.

'Then might you have been mistaken in what you saw?'

Jos, in some confusion, launched into a ramble in which he denied that he drank to excess, and claimed that in any case he was perfectly able to hold his drink and that his eyesight and memory had been unaffected by what he had taken that day. Sir Benjamin did not press the point, for there was no need to, and Jos was allowed to step down, which he did thankfully.

By way of demonstrating the reliability of Jos's memory (for there was no other reason to debate the matter in such detail given that the man who had threatened Davie could, unfortunately, not be produced), the defence then recalled Inspector Scott, who confirmed that three gloves had been found in the dead man's pockets: one pair in tan suède, with the name of a popular American glove-maker on the label, and one single glove in dark-grey kidskin of a slightly smaller size, which had no label at all. On further questioning, Inspector Scott agreed that it looked rather as though the odd glove did not belong to David Marchmont, but said that they had not attempted to trace its owner for it had not been thought necessary. Anyone might accidentally pick up an odd glove, he said, and the police had had no reason to consider it suspicious so had given it no further thought.

As Scott gave his evidence, something stirred in Freddy's mind and he frowned. What was it that had occurred to him just then? Someone had been talking to him about gloves recently, he was sure of it. He racked his brain for a few seconds but nothing came to him. It was a pity, for he had the oddest feeling that it might be important, but there was no use in chasing a fleeting thought, and so he shrugged and abandoned the effort. Perhaps it would come to him later.

The next witnesses were Samuel and Ernest Hepworth, two lively-looking lads of fourteen and thirteen, who were something of a triumph of Freddy's, for he had had great difficulty in finding them and persuading them to speak.

They were brothers who lived in Chalfont St. Giles, they said, and had been staying with an elderly aunt in South Audley Street for a few days at the time of the murder, for there was a nasty outbreak of whooping cough at school and the healthy ones had all been sent away until it passed. It was evident that this aunt of theirs had no idea how to manage them and even less idea of what they had been getting up to while they were guests under her roof, for as Mr. Travers questioned them gently it became clear that they had pretty much run wild from the day of their arrival until the day they had returned to school.

It was, of course, the week of the fifth of November, and the brothers had built up quite a collection of fireworks, which they took particular glee in setting off at every opportunity, much to the annoyance of the neighbours. On the Sunday they were due to return to school, and so on the Saturday they slipped out of the house late at night with the intention of holding a firework display in the street for their own private enjoyment, using what remained of their collection. In order to avoid having to suffer inconvenient and tiresome remonstrance from their aunt if she discovered them, they went around the corner to Mount Street to do it. To their disappointment, it turned out that most of the fireworks had somehow got damp, but they did manage to cause enough disturbance to give them satisfaction and to make them agree that it had certainly been worth while. They then crept back into the house and returned to school the next day, with nobody being any the wiser.

It was evident as they stood in the witness-box that they were worried they would get into trouble, but Mr. Travers did his best to reassure them that the case was quite the opposite, and that they were doing the right thing by appearing today, for their evidence might well save a woman's life. At this they looked suitably impressed and straightened up, waiting for the questions to begin.

'Now, Sam,' said Mr. Travers to the eldest boy. 'Do you remember exactly at what time you began letting off the fireworks?'

'Not exactly, sir, no,' said Sam. 'It was late.'

'Well, then, do you remember whether it was before or after midnight?'

Sam looked at his brother and they both said together, 'After midnight.'

'You are sure of that?'

'Yes, sir,' said Sam. 'We set an alarm clock to go off at twelve o'clock. Aunt goes to bed at half past eleven, and we thought that would give her enough time to fall asleep.'

'Very good,' said Mr. Travers. 'Now, you say that when you arrived in Mount Street you swiftly discovered that most of your fireworks had got damp—not surprising, of course, for it had been raining heavily that week. Can you tell us how many dry ones were left?'

Sam screwed up his face to think but Ernest spoke up immediately.

'Nine or ten,' he said. 'There was a rocket and three penny Roman candles, and a few whizz-bangs.'

'Whizz-bangs?' said Mr. Travers.

'Yes. They go "whizz-bang,"' said Ernest, as though it were obvious.

Here there was an appreciative chuckle from the court, and Mr. Travers said, 'Ah, yes, of course. Now, I don't suppose you remember which one you let off first?'

'The rocket,' said Sam promptly.

'The rocket,' repeated Mr. Travers. 'And did it make a loud bang?'

'I'll say,' said Ernest, and they both giggled.

'And what came after that?'

'The Roman candles,' said Sam.

'Did they make a noise?'

'Not to speak of,' said Sam. 'They fizzed a bit, but not very loudly.'

'Then after that came the—er—whizz-bangs, yes?'

They nodded.

'And did they make the noise you expected?'

'No,' said Ernest in disgust. 'They whizzed all right, but they hardly banged at all.'

'They hardly banged at all? Are you quite certain of that?' said Mr. Travers.

'Yes, sir,' said Sam, nodding. 'They made a bit of noise, but it was more of a crackle than a bang.'

'So, then,' said Mr. Travers, who had maintained a straight face throughout. 'Just to be sure I have got this correct, you set *all* the fireworks off after midnight, and only one of them made a loud bang. The others merely fizzed or crackled.'

'That's right, sir,' said Sam.

'Did you hear any other fireworks while you were in Mount Street? Or any other bangs?'

'No, sir,' they said.

Sir Benjamin had no questions and they were allowed to go, looking somewhat relieved that they were not to be locked up immediately. Mr. Travers hoped that he had planted a seed of doubt into the jury's mind as to the time of the killing, for if the noises Mrs. Trumpington had heard after midnight were all fireworks, then the bang she had heard at just after ten o'clock must have been the sound of the gun going off, and for that time Angela Marchmont had an alibi.

The court then adjourned for lunch, and everybody filed out in pleasant anticipation of what was to come, for they knew that the defence case would continue that afternoon with the testimony of Angela Marchmont herself, and all were curious to hear what the prisoner would have to say.

Sure enough, when they returned, the clerk called for Mrs. Angela Marchmont to take the oath, which she duly did. Alas for the dedicated pursuit of justice, Mr. Travers got no further than asking her to confirm her name before a juror was assailed by a fit of such explosive sneezing that proceedings were halted for a minute to allow him to recover. The sneezing was, however, followed immediately by a copious and impressive nose-bleed—an affliction to which the man was particularly prone, he explained. Handkerchiefs were brought out and handed along, but by that time the unfortunate juror was a gory sight, and one of the female jury members had begun to feel faint at the sight of the blood and asked if she might go home. Seeing that things were getting out of hand, the judge suggested that they adjourn for the day and return refreshed on Monday, since the prisoner herself was about to give important evidence and it was vital that the jury be in a frame of mind to concentrate on what she said.

So the court was cleared and everybody went about their business. As for Angela, she returned to prison in the full expectation that next week she would be found guilty and sentenced to hang. It was not a pleasant prospect, but she had had many years' practice in the matter of suppressing unpleasant thoughts, so she appeared as calm as ever, and to look at her no-one would have ever supposed that she had anything particularly inconvenient to look forward to.

CHAPTER NINETEEN

JUST AS SAM and Ernest were stepping into the witness-box to regale the court with their tales of mischief, anyone who happened to be observing the press bench at the time might have seen Freddy Pilkington-Soames glance around the court and suddenly fix his attention on something. He raised his eyebrows at whatever it was and seemed to indicate towards the door, then turned to whisper in Kathie's ear. She nodded and looked round, and Freddy rose and crept out of the place as quietly as possible, leaving Kathie in the company of Harry, the old reporter with the collection of pencils, who had taken a liking to Mrs. Jameson over the past week—not least because she was married to a Scotland Yard inspector and might thus be a useful source of news.

Freddy emerged from the Old Bailey and looked about him. It was a frosty day and people hurried to and fro, huddled up inside their coat collars. To his right a young woman was walking briskly up the street. He followed her at a discreet distance as she crossed over Newgate Street and entered a church. Freddy waited a minute and then entered too. Marthe was sitting in a pew not far from the door, apparently engaged in quiet contemplation of the rather magnificent stained glass window above the altar. Freddy joined her and they sat in silence for some moments.

At last, without looking at him, she said, 'Madame gave me notice this morning.'

'Oh?' said Freddy, surprised.

'Yes. She said she knew my loyalty could not be doubted, but that she did not want me to disadvantage myself by waiting until the last minute to find a new situation, and so she has released me from her service with immediate effect. William she has also dismissed.'

'Goodness me,' said Freddy. 'If she's letting you go then that must mean she doesn't hold out much hope of getting off.'

Marthe bowed her head.

'I fear that is so,' she said. 'And can you blame her? I have sat in the court every day and heard them shame and humiliate her. They make it sound as though she were wicked and sinful, when I know she is nothing of the sort. They taunt her for the mistakes she made in the past, and say she was so desperate to get rid of her husband that she killed him. But people kill out of love or hate. Madame neither loved him nor hated him. She cared nothing for him any more. Then why should she kill him? I will not believe it.'

'I don't believe it either,' said Freddy. 'But then who *did* do it?'

'I do not know,' said Marthe. 'I was not there. Had I not gone to France then none of this would have happened.'

There was bitterness in her tone, and Freddy regarded her sympathetically. Then she turned to him, and her next words surprised him.

'I can do nothing about the past, but perhaps I can help her now,' she said. 'She told me not to give her away and I swore I should never betray her trust, even if it meant I had to stand by and break my heart as she let herself go to the gallows. But now that she has released me from her service, I am free to do as I please and need no longer keep silent.'

She gave him a look that dared him to contradict her.

'I suppose that is true,' he said after a moment. 'Does that mean you have something to tell me about all this?'

She hesitated, as though still debating whether to speak.

'I know the name of the man you saw with Madame on the night of her husband's death,' she said at last. 'At least, I think I do. He came to see Madame on the day I went away, and I imagine it was he you saw.'

'Who is he?' said Freddy, and held his breath as he waited for her reply.

'His name is Edgar Valencourt,' she said. 'He has many other aliases, but that is the one by which Madame knows him.'

'Edgar Valencourt?' said Freddy with a frown. 'I seem to recognize the name.'

'Yes. That is because he is wanted by the police,' said Marthe in a matter-of-fact voice.

Freddy stared.

'Good Lord!' he exclaimed. 'Yes, I remember now. I've heard of him. He frequents the watering-places of Continental Europe, relieving elderly foreign duchesses of their tiaras and other superfluous trinkets. What on earth is Angela doing mixing with his sort? Has she quite taken leave of her senses? I should have thought she'd have better taste than that.'

'She is in love with him,' said Marthe, as though that explained everything.

'I should hope so,' said Freddy, 'because otherwise she has no excuse at all for being such a fathead. Where did she meet him?'

'In Cornwall,' said Marthe. 'But she fell in love with him in Italy.'

'Ah!' said Freddy, remembering a certain conversation last summer. 'Well, I only hope she counted her loose change before she came away. A criminal, of all people! What the devil can she have been thinking of?'

'He makes her happy,' said Marthe. 'And he is charming—far more charming than her husband, who blackmailed her and was unfaithful.'

'Well, I suppose even a jewel-thief would seem like a catch after that foul excrescence,' said Freddy. 'Poor Angela. And so you think she was with this Valencourt fellow on the night of the murder? No wonder she refused to tell anybody where she was. She could hardly use him as an alibi, could she? What choice did she have but to claim that she spent the night in her own bed, even though she knew it was a thin story? Why, none at all! I see now why she kept quiet. I say,' he went on suddenly. 'It doesn't really help us to know this, does it? I mean, it's not as though we can go and fetch the fellow and insist he come and give evidence in court. He's hardly going to look upon the request too favourably if he's on the run, is he? I don't suppose you know where he is, by the way?'

'I know where he might be,' said Marthe. 'That is why I came to you. You are right when you say that he is not the best person on whom to rely. Even if he agrees to come and speak in court to say that they were together that night—which is by no means certain, for they will arrest him immediately—still people will not believe that Madame is innocent. All they will say then is that the two of them did the murder together, and that she is worse than they already believed her to be. And yet—and yet somehow I *know* he can help.'

'But how?'

'I cannot tell. Perhaps someone saw them together, or perhaps he has some piece of evidence that will prove Madame was not in the flat when her husband died—I do not know, but I am certain that he is our only hope now.' She turned to him and fixed him with a fierce stare. 'You say we cannot go and fetch him, M. Pilkington-Soames, but I say that if it is Madame's only chance then we *must* do it.'

Freddy had never seen the girl so animated, and at that moment he could not doubt her devotion to her mistress.

'You're right, of course,' he said. 'It's the least we can do for Angela. Where is he, then? You said you knew.'

'There is a little town just outside Rheims,' said Marthe. 'I used to go and stay with my cousins there when I was a girl. M. Valencourt told me he knew the town well, and was planning to go there soon himself. Whether he went, or whether he is still there after all this time I cannot say, but it is all the information I have, and I should never forgive myself if I did not at least *try* to find him. I should like your help, but if you will not come then I will go myself and *make* him come back one way or another.'

'Of course I'll come with you,' said Freddy, who was only too keen to be doing something.

'Good,' said Marthe. 'But we must go immediately, for there is no time to lose. William will come with us.'

She nodded over her shoulder as she spoke, and Freddy turned to see the young American, who had just then come into the church and was looking at Marthe inquiringly.

'He says he will come,' said Marthe to William.

William nodded.

'Good,' he said. 'I don't mind tackling him by myself, but if we have to bring him back by force then the more the merrier, I reckon.'

'I hope it won't come to that,' said Freddy. 'Still, you may rely on me to do what I can.'

'Then let's go,' said William.

CHAPTER TWENTY

THERE WAS A thin layer of snow on the ground, and dusk was falling when they finally saw a sign for Rheims and knew they were approaching their destination. They had been mostly silent throughout the journey, for each of them knew what a desperate and probably futile venture it was. Although Valencourt had mentioned a certain house to Marthe and she thought she knew where it was, the chances of finding him there were slim, to say the least, and had it not been for the fact that Angela's life depended on it, they would never have dreamed of setting out on the journey at all.

Under Marthe's instructions they turned off the road a few miles before they reached the city, and headed East. Here, the countryside was flat and barren, and the snow patchy and muddy, and the motor-car bumped along unfamiliar country roads bounded by vast fields, passing through the occasional hamlet or small village. At one point they stopped to allow Marthe to ask for directions, and then turned around and headed back the way they had come.

'It is a long time since I was here,' explained Marthe.

For a few minutes it looked as though they would not be able to find the place at all, then they saw a half-concealed sign that pointed to the right, and Marthe gave an exclamation of satisfaction.

'That way,' she said.

After a few minutes they saw that they were passing through the main street of a large village. Few people were about, since everything was closed for the day, and lights glimmered out of the windows of the houses round about. Soon they left the village behind them, and Marthe began to look about her.

'There,' she said suddenly.

To their left they could dimly see through the dusk the outline of what looked like a large farmhouse, which stood about a hundred yards back from the road.

'We had better stop here,' she said.

William drew the car up and they all climbed out. The house was at the end of a long track, and they regarded it warily. As far as they could see, there were no lights at the windows.

'Well, there's no use in our coming all the way here for nothing,' said Freddy at last, and started up the path. The other two followed, and soon they were standing before a solid wooden front door mounted with a black knocker.

'What do we do now?' whispered William.

They hesitated for a moment, then with an impatient noise Marthe stepped forward and rapped on the door sharply. They waited, but no-one came. She rapped again.

'It was always a slim hope,' said Freddy, after a minute. 'Now what?'

William had wandered off and was peering through windows. He disappeared around the side of the house and Freddy looked at his watch.

'Perhaps we ought to come back and try again tomorrow,' he said, 'although I don't suppose he's here.'

Just then, William rejoined them in a hurry.

'There's a light at the back of the house,' he said in a whisper, and motioned to them to follow him.

A path led around to the back, where they could dimly see what looked like a kitchen garden, bare and forlorn in the freezing cold of January. Freddy and Marthe followed William and saw that he had been speaking the truth, for as soon as they got there they saw a pool of faint light issuing from one of the windows. Freddy peered in cautiously, and saw that the light came from a candle set on a wooden table in the centre of a neat little kitchen.

'There must be someone here, then,' whispered Freddy. 'What shall we do? He won't answer the door.'

'I say we wait until he's gone to bed and then break in,' said William.

'But what if we've got the wrong house?' said Freddy.

'Then we apologize and pay for breakages,' said William. 'Either that, or we spend the next few weeks in gaol.'

'Splendid,' said Freddy. 'A spell in a French prison? I can't think of anything I'd like better.'

Marthe was already heading back towards the front of the house. The other two followed, and for the next few hours they sat huddled in the car, waiting until they thought there was a good chance that whoever lived in the house had gone to bed. At last, when the dusk had long turned pitch black and the lights of the distant village had been extinguished one by one, they emerged and set off up the path to the lonely house once again. There was no longer a light in the kitchen, and the place was in darkness, but fortunately William had thought to bring a torch, and so they were not entirely helpless.

They had agreed that the most likely entry-place was a window to the side of the house, which gave into a little scullery. When they reached it, Freddy removed his coat and held it against the glass in order to dampen the sound as much as possible, and then William gave the window a sharp blow with the heel of the torch. The glass gave immediately, and they all caught their breath at the sound it made as it hit the scullery floor with a loud tinkle. Nobody came, however, and after a few moments Freddy reached inside and loosened the window catch.

'Better let me go first,' whispered William, who came from a family of acrobats. In a trice he was up on the sill and through the window.

'Go around to the front and wait for us,' said Freddy to Marthe, who had refused absolutely to stay in the car. He climbed up and followed William through the window with slightly more difficulty.

It was pitch dark in the scullery. William switched on the torch and led the way out and into a stone-flagged passage lined with doors. He opened the first one. It creaked loudly and they held their breath for an age, it seemed, but nobody came. William glanced in and shone the torch around briefly, then shook his head. They looked quickly into the other rooms but found no-one. Presumably the lighter of the candle had retired upstairs to bed. William glanced at Freddy and indicated upwards with his head. Freddy nodded and put a foot on the bottom stair.

'You won't find anyone up there,' said a voice, and they whirled around to find themselves caught in the bright beam of another torch, which blinded them and prevented them from seeing who was speaking. Whoever it was must have approached as silently as a cat, for they had not heard a thing, and evidently he did not appreciate finding two strangers in his house late at night, for his voice sounded distinctly unamused.

'Who's that?' said Freddy, somewhat idiotically in the circumstances.

There was a pause, then the voice said:

'I know you, don't I? Look here, what's all this?'

The torch went off and there was the hiss of a gas lamp being lit, and suddenly the place was illuminated and they saw they were standing in the entrance passage of the house. Before them stood Edgar Valencourt, in his shirt sleeves but otherwise fully dressed. He looked from one of them to the other, his expression grim. They were not looking at his face, however, but at the gun which he held in his hand.

'I think you'd better explain yourselves,' he said.

CHAPTER TWENTY-ONE

FREDDY EYED THE gun warily. This was certainly the man who had been dancing with Angela, and he did not look especially pleased to see them.

'Must you point that thing at us?' he said. 'We only wanted to talk to you.'

'That's obvious enough,' said Valencourt. 'Most people who knock and get no answer take the hint and go away instead of breaking in through the scullery. But as you can see, I'm not accepting visitors at present.'

At that moment there was a loud rapping at the door, and he glanced back but did not lower the gun.

'It's Marthe,' said William. 'She's seen us and wants to come in.'

'Marthe?' said Valencourt in astonishment. He regarded the two young men for a second, then, reaching a sudden decision, tucked the gun in his belt and went to fling open the door. Immediately Marthe pushed past him and into the house.

'Look here, what the devil is all this?' demanded Valencourt.

'I take it you don't know,' said Freddy, but got no further before Marthe turned to Valencourt and burst into a torrent of voluble and excited French. He stared as though he could not believe his ears.

'*What?*' he exclaimed, and had they had any doubts as to his ignorance of Angela's plight before, they were now dispelled, for it was perfectly evident that this was wholly unexpected news to him. 'Is this a joke?' he said, looking from one to the other of them. 'It's not very funny if it is.'

'*Non,*' said Marthe, shaking her head vigorously. 'M. Pilkington-Soames, he will tell you.'

'I only wish it were a joke,' said Freddy. 'But do you really suppose we came all the way to France and broke into your house just for the fun of it? We wanted to speak to you. Angela's in the devil of a fix and they're almost certain to hang her if she can't prove she was somewhere else that night, and yet she won't even try.'

'What do you mean, she won't even try?' said Valencourt.

Freddy now told him briefly about Davie Marchmont's death, and about the trial, and how bad things looked for Angela, and Valencourt listened. The wary look had now returned to his face, and aside from that first exclamation of surprise at the news, nobody could have said what was passing through his mind.

'And what has all this to do with me?' he said, when Freddy had finished.

'You were with her that night, weren't you?' said Freddy.

'What makes you think that?' said Valencourt. 'Did Angela tell you?'

'No, of course not,' said Freddy. 'She won't say a word. She insists she was at home all night and didn't notice her husband's body behind the sofa until the morning, but I saw you together at the White Rabbit Ball and I drew my own conclusions. I don't know where the two of you were, although I'm pretty sure it wasn't her flat, but for some reason the silly woman won't give you away even to save her own skin.'

'Won't she?' said Valencourt. For a second an odd, indefinable look passed across his face, but it vanished quickly and his expression once again became unreadable.

'You must come, *monsieur*,' said Marthe. 'If you tell them that she was with you that night then they will let her go and she will be safe.'

'Are you quite certain of that, though?' said Valencourt. 'I rather think Angela has got it right. It seems to me that my interference is likely to make things worse, if anything. I suppose you know I'm not exactly a favourite of the police. If I step forward and say Angela was with me—and mind, I'm not admitting she was—then the court is hardly going to look favourably upon her, is it? Our having been together that night won't do her reputation any good at all. And in any case, leaving aside the small matter of the various warrants for my arrest—which may be unimportant to you, but which I can't quite bring myself to ignore—I can't prove where I was that night either. It seems to me that if I come forward all that will happen is that they'll say we were in it together and hang two of us instead of one, and that would be rather a waste, don't you think?'

Freddy's heart sank, for it looked as though Valencourt would refuse to come back with them, just as he had feared. They had only ever had a slim hope of finding him and persuading him to do it, but to have got this far only to fall at the last fence was almost too much to bear. Of course, it was hardly likely that a hardened criminal would be prepared to sacrifice himself for someone else—especially a woman he had probably considered as a mere plaything—but still, Freddy had hoped that he might have been willing to help them in some way. If he were not, then all hope was gone. Perhaps he might be persuaded to give them a signed statement. It would be better than nothing.

Marthe was by no means discouraged, however.

'You are right, *monsieur,*' she said, 'and if we could have found any other way to do it, then we should not have come to you. But somehow I know you can help if you only will. You do not wish to see her hanged, surely?'

'Of course I don't,' said Valencourt. 'But you must see that it's useless for me to try and provide her with an alibi. Nobody saw us, and the jury will never take my word for it once they find out who I am.'

'But you are all we have,' she said. 'If you care for Madame at all, then please help us. Please, *monsieur.*'

He looked at her beseeching face.

'Is there really no hope that she'll be acquitted?' he said.

'None at all, barring some miracle,' said Freddy. 'The prosecution has a very strong case indeed. They know he was killed with her gun, and they know—or at least they *think* they know—that she was in the flat at the time he died. And they've made it look as though she had every reason to do it. If it were anybody else but Angela I'd be convinced myself that she did it. Oh yes, they'll find her guilty all right—there's not a doubt of it.'

'I see,' said Valencourt, and still his expression was closed so that they had no idea of his thoughts. They waited. 'Tell me exactly what happened,' he said at last. 'Perhaps I can do something, but I shall need to know all about it first. As you've probably realized, I don't get the newspapers delivered here, so this has all caught me rather unprepared.'

'I brought this week's papers with me,' said Freddy. 'They're in the car.'

'I'll get them,' said William.

'I've been reporting the case myself,' went on Freddy after William had gone out. 'It's been pretty sick-making, I don't mind telling you. Poor Angela's been having the devil of a time.'

'Has she?' said Valencourt, and again the odd look passed briefly across his face. He hesitated and said, almost as though he were unwilling to ask, 'How is she bearing up?'

'Very well, considering that she's had to listen to all her private concerns being talked about and judged in front of hundreds of people. It seems she has a daughter nobody knew about, and her husband was blackmailing her over it. Hardly the kind of thing one wants to talk about before strangers.'

'A daughter?' said Valencourt in surprise. 'Barbara,' he said after a moment's thought.

'Yes. Did you know?' said Freddy.

'Not at all,' said Valencourt, 'but I've met the young lady in question, and they do look very alike. I ought to have realized at the time. Look here,' he went on as William returned with the newspapers, 'we're cluttering up the house by standing in this passage. You'd better come into the parlour while I read. You see, even someone of my sort knows how to treat his guests,' he said ironically to William, who had hardly spoken a word, but who somehow managed to radiate dislike for Valencourt even while remaining perfectly respectful.

They followed him into the parlour and sat as he read the newspaper reports carefully, only pausing now and again to ask Freddy a question. He seemed particularly interested in what Alfred Pearson had said about Davie Marchmont that day at Burkett's. At last he threw down the latest edition of the *Clarion* and looked up.

'It all looks rather bad for her, doesn't it?' he said. 'Does the defence have anything else?'

'Not much,' said Freddy. 'We can throw some doubt on the time of the gunshot, but most of the case rests on this mysterious foreigner who was seen threatening Marchmont on the day he died.'

'Ah, yes,' said Valencourt non-committally and gazed at the floor as though he were thinking.

They waited in silence, hardly daring to look at one another. Would he agree to help them? He was their last hope, and without him Angela would almost certainly die. In the silence a clock ticked loudly, reminding them all of how little time they had left. Valencourt had raised his head and was now looking unseeingly at the wall. His face gradually assumed a grim expression, and for the first time he seemed to be undergoing some sort of internal struggle.

'Damn the woman!' he exclaimed suddenly. 'Can't she be left alone for an instant without getting herself into trouble?' He sighed and looked around at the others. 'Well, I suppose there's no help for it. I shall have to come back.'

'Then you will tell everybody she was with you that night?' said Marthe.

'No. I've already said there's no use at all in my trying to give her an alibi,' said Valencourt. 'I've thought about it and I can't see how it would help.'

'Then you're just going to abandon her?' said Freddy.

'I didn't say that,' said Valencourt. 'But I can't do what you want me to do.' He held up a hand as Marthe looked about to burst into speech. 'I said I might be able to help, but you must let me do things my own way and not ask questions. Promise me that.'

He looked around at the three of them. They glanced at one another and nodded, and he seemed satisfied.

'Very good,' he said. 'Now, this is going to be rather tricky so it's vitally important that you say nothing to anyone of what has been said here tonight. If anyone finds out that we talked of this beforehand then my coming forward will do more harm than good. You must keep quiet. Is that agreed?'

They all nodded.

'Very well. Furthermore, you'll have to trust me to give myself up. I shall go to this Travers first and speak to him, and then after that I dare say he'll want to hand me over to the police.'

'You'll come back with us, though?' said Freddy.

'Yes, but we mustn't arrive together. It must look as though I am doing this of my own volition.'

'But how do we know you won't run off when we get to London?' said William.

'You don't,' said Valencourt. 'But if I wanted to run off I should have done so by now—should have done it hours ago, in fact, when the three of you started thundering about like a herd of elephants in my back garden.'

'Why didn't you?' said Freddy curiously.

'Because you drew so much attention to yourselves that I knew you couldn't possibly be dangerous,' said Valencourt. 'Besides, I was planning to leave tomorrow and preferred to spend the last night in my own bed rather than running about the countryside in the freezing cold and dark.'

'If you were going to leave tomorrow then it is a good thing we came when we did,' said Marthe.

'Yes, it is,' said Valencourt. 'For you, at least; less so for me. Now, another thing: none of you must say a word to Angela about this. She mustn't know a thing about it. If she has refused to give me away all this time then she won't be any too pleased to hear that I'm planning to appear as a witness. She might even forbid Travers from allowing it.'

'Not if she knows what's good for her,' said Freddy.

'Well, from what you say, obviously she doesn't,' said Valencourt dryly. He looked at his watch. 'Now, it's getting late so I suggest we all turn in, as we'll need to get an early start if we're going to be ready by Monday morning. You needn't worry,' he said to William, who looked as though he did not like this idea, 'I won't run off in the night.'

'I'd like to believe it,' said William, 'but I'd hate to think we'd come all the way here for nothing.'

Valencourt sighed.

'Oh, very well, then. You're evidently determined not to trust me, and I don't say I blame you. Suppose you lock me in my room tonight. Will that do?'

'It would do better if you'd hand over that gun,' said Freddy.

'No, I don't think I will,' said Valencourt thoughtfully. 'It was given to me so I could protect myself, and I have the feeling it might come in useful very soon. Don't worry, I won't fire it—as a matter of fact, it's in Angela's interests that I don't.'

And with that they were forced to be content. It was now almost two o'clock, so they all rose and Valencourt led them upstairs and indicated two little bedrooms that they might use.

'I am sorry you will have to give yourself up and be arrested,' said Marthe, before he was locked into his own room.

'I've had ten years longer than I expected to get,' he said. 'It was bound to happen sooner or later. I dare say it doesn't matter much any more.'

'Still, I thank you,' said Marthe. 'We are very grateful for it, and I hope Madame will be too.'

He gave a wry smile.

'I don't think she will, Marthe,' he said. 'In fact, I don't suppose she'll be very pleased at all when she hears what I have to say.'

And with that he shut the door and they turned the key on him.

CHAPTER TWENTY-TWO

ON MONDAY MORNING the usual crowd flocked into the court-room at the Old Bailey, eager to hear what Mrs. Marchmont would have to say for herself today after proceedings had been so rudely cut short on Friday. Freddy and Kathie were once more in their seats on the press bench. Kathie wanted to know why Freddy had left so suddenly on Friday, but he shook his head mysteriously and put a finger over his lips.

'Shh!' he said. 'Mustn't tell. I think there are going to be a few surprises this morning, though.'

In reality he was by no means certain that this was the case. They had brought Edgar Valencourt to London on Saturday morning and left him outside the chambers of Mr. Travers. They had then waited some little distance away and watched as he was admitted and disappeared out of sight, and that was the last they had seen of him. As the ever-suspicious William said, there was no saying that he had not gone in and then run straight out again through another door, but Marthe shook her head and said she was sure he would never do such a thing to Madame—and besides, he might have escaped at any time before that; there was no need at all for him to have come to London with them. And so they were forced to wait and hope that Valencourt had kept his word, and that whatever he had to say to Mr. Travers would do some good and perhaps turn the tide of fortune in Angela's favour at last. Freddy hoped that Angela would not be too angry with him when she found out what he had done, but even if she were he would never regret having done it—for if, out of some misplaced sense of loyalty, she would not do anything to save herself, then she must be saved against her will; there was nothing else for it.

As for Angela, she was becoming increasingly weary and hopeless. She had sat in silence for most of the weekend, and had even begun to toy with the idea of admitting to the murder, just to get it all over and done with, for whether she confessed or not it all came down to the same thing in the end. At least if she were to admit to it then she could dispense with the trouble of having to sit in court for the next day or two, looking on as learned gentlemen crowned with horsehair treated her plight as though it were an amusing intellectual conundrum to be solved, and debated calmly as to whether she deserved to live or not. How many more innocent people throughout history had been tempted to do the same thing, Angela wondered. She had only ever observed the machinery of the law from the side of the acknowledged righteous, but now she was seeing it from the other side, and over the past weeks she had learnt that there was something about being exposed to the judgment of the nation which tended to crush the spirit somewhat. Even when she received a hurried note from Mr. Travers on Sunday, hinting at some new evidence that would change everything, she felt no joy at the prospect, for by now she was almost certain that the jury had already made up its mind and that it was too late to change it. Perhaps it would be easier to let the law do what it would and try to forget the inevitable consequences.

Such were her thoughts as she was led into the dock on Monday morning. As she glanced around the court-room, however, she caught sight of Freddy and Kathie in their usual spot on the press bench, and took heart. They had sat there throughout the proceedings, giving her encouraging looks and smiles whenever she happened to turn her head in their direction and doing their best to let her know that whatever anyone else thought, they believed her, at least. William and Marthe, too, had sat loyally through it all, reminding her that she still had friends who wished the best for her. Angela took a deep breath and straightened up. She felt no more hopeful about her prospects at the sight of them all, but neither would she crumble in their presence, for her pride would not allow it. She would remain courageous and keep a cool head to the bitter end, she was determined.

This was a fine resolution, but she almost broke it as soon as proceedings began. She had expected to be called to continue giving evidence on her own behalf, but instead there was a pause as Mr. Travers approached the bench and murmured something to the judge. Sir Benjamin was summoned to join in the conversation, and there was much nodding and consulting of papers. At last they seemed to reach agreement, and all returned to their proper places. Still the clerk did not call for her, but instead called out something else—someone's name, she thought. The spectators in the public gallery were still shuffling at the delay and someone was having a loud coughing fit as he spoke, and so Angela did not hear it properly. But there was no mistaking the familiar figure of the man who stepped into the witness-box a minute later. Angela's heart gave a great thump as she saw him and she drew in a silent breath, but she exerted herself to remain composed and so, other than the fact that her face had gone a little paler, nobody could have known by looking at her that she had any particular opinion about this new witness, for she gave him only one quick glance and then cast her eyes downward as though uninterested in what he might have to say. In reality, of course, her mind and her heart were in turmoil, and she knew not whether to feel dismay or relief at Edgar Valencourt's arrival. She had done her best not to bring him into the thing, knowing that it would mean certain arrest for him without any likely benefit for her, but now it looked as though her efforts had been all for nothing, since he had come forward anyway. Now everybody would know that she had been consorting with a criminal—although after what had been revealed about her during the course of the trial, she did not suppose anyone could possibly think worse of her than they already did. Still, there was some comfort to be had from the fact that he had cared enough about her to come forward. She would cling to that thought and hope for the best.

The people in the public gallery perked up with interest when they saw the new witness, for here was someone unexpected, and they sensed an exciting revelation was about to occur. For his part, Valencourt, dressed smartly and soberly, stood in the witness-box, seemingly quite at ease with himself, and waited politely for Mr. Travers to begin, which he duly did.

'You are Edgar Valencourt?' he said.

'I am,' said Valencourt.

'You came to see me on Saturday and told me that you had important new information about the death of David Marchmont,' said Mr. Travers. 'Mr. Marchmont was killed in November. If you intended to come forward, why did you not do it then?'

'I have been out of the country for the past two months, and knew nothing of the court case,' said Valencourt. 'It was only when I happened to pick up an English newspaper on Friday that I found out about it. Otherwise I should have done it long before now.'

'I see. Then it is perhaps fortunate for Mrs. Marchmont that you are here,' said Mr. Travers. He glanced down at a paper he was holding in his hand, then resumed. 'Now, you go by the name of Edgar Valencourt. Are you the same Edgar Valencourt who is currently being sought by the police with respect to a number of jewel-thefts which have taken place over the past few years in various countries?'

'Yes.'

'I see. Might I ask whether the name you are using at present is your real one?'

'It is part of it, but it is not my full name.'

'Then what is your full name?'

'Edgar Valencourt de Lisle.'

'Edgar Valencourt de Lisle,' repeated Mr. Travers. 'And is this the first time you have appeared before an English court in any capacity?'

'No, it is not. I appeared before Maidstone Assizes about ten years ago in the capacity of defendant.'

'Oh?' said Mr. Travers, as Valencourt fell silent. 'And what was the nature of the offence with which you were charged?'

For the first time Valencourt looked uncomfortable. He hesitated and seemed reluctant to speak. Mr. Travers, who was not about to let victory elude him now that it was within his grasp, decided to give him a prompt. His voice now rang out, and what he had to say sounded harsh and stark in the silent court-room.

'Let me help you. Are you or are you not the same Edgar de Lisle who was found guilty of the murder of his wife, Selina de Lisle, in July of nineteen eighteen?'

Angela glanced up sharply, then back down again. Her heart had begun to beat rapidly, and she was conscious of a rushing of blood in her ears and a sudden light-headedness. She gripped the edge of the dock tightly to steady herself.

Valencourt, looking straight ahead, said quietly after a moment:

'I am.'

There was a brief stir which was swiftly hushed up. Now the judge addressed Mr. Travers.

'Is this true?' he said.

'Yes, my lord,' said Mr. Travers. 'You may remember the murder, since it was reported rather widely at the time.'

'I believe I do,' said the judge. 'A most serious case. Still, that is not the matter under discussion at present. Please carry on.'

Mr. Travers turned back to Valencourt.

'You escaped from prison during a disturbance before the sentence of execution could be carried out, I believe?' he said.

'Yes, I did,' replied Valencourt.

'And you have managed to elude the police all this time?'

'It appears so,' said Valencourt.

'Then why have you come forward now? What is it that you wish to tell us about this case?'

'Only that I know the prisoner to be innocent of the crime with which she has been charged. I know she did not kill David Marchmont.'

'Oh? And how exactly do you know that?'

'Because I killed him myself,' said Valencourt.

CHAPTER TWENTY-THREE

A T THAT A tumult broke out which could not be contained for some minutes. As the court officials did their
best to maintain order, Edgar Valencourt continued to look
straight ahead of him, apparently unmoved by the sensation
he had created—not least among three of the spectators, who
had had not the faintest idea that this was coming. Freddy's jaw
dropped, and he looked across at Marthe and William, who
were staring at one another, dumbfounded. The revelation
of Valencourt's previous conviction for murder was surprise
enough, but this was even more astonishing. They had expected him to give Angela some sort of alibi—perhaps a false
one that did not reveal the true nature of their relationship—
but they had never dreamed that he would go to the lengths
of confessing to the murder. Kathie was frantically nudging
Freddy in the ribs, and he glanced towards Angela, who looked
as though she did not quite know where she was. As they
watched, they saw her visibly pull herself together, although
her hands still rested on the edge of the dock as if for support.

When calm was finally restored, the questioning continued.

'That is a surprising confession to make, Mr. Valencourt,' said Mr. Travers. 'Especially in view of the fact that we are here today to try someone else entirely for the crime in question. Can you support your assertion with evidence?'

'Yes, I can,' said Valencourt.

'Then will you tell us of the circumstances which led to your killing David Marchmont?'

'Certainly. I met David Marchmont on the seventh of November last, in some bar or other in Soho—I don't recall the name. We were playing cards in a private room late at night, and he subbed me when I nearly lost everything after making a silly mistake, which saved me from losing a pretty large sum. He rather attached himself to me after that, and since I was grateful to him I didn't object. We spent a couple of nights going to various places to play and very soon I found myself subbing *him*, although he promised to pay me back. After a day or two I began to realize I'd made a mistake and that he was the sort of fellow who liked to latch on to people and take advantage of them. By Friday he owed me rather a lot of money, and since I knew he was in funds by then I asked him when he was going to pay me, but he laughed and made some excuse and said he'd pay me the next day. On Saturday I met him at his club and we had words outside, which I gather were overheard.'

'Did you drop a glove when you spoke to Mr. Marchmont that day?' said Mr. Travers.

'I think I must have. I didn't notice it at the time, but I missed it later.'

A glove was produced and handed to the witness.

'Is this it?'

'It looks very like it,' said Valencourt.

'This is the glove that was found in the pocket of David Marchmont,' said Mr. Travers to the jury. 'We have here also another glove which Mr. Valencourt gave me on Saturday. Please be so good as to examine the two gloves.'

The jury did so. They were quite clearly a pair. Mr. Travers invited Valencourt to continue.

'I hadn't intended to see the fellow again but that evening I bumped into him, and against my better judgment agreed to go for a drink with him, as he said he wanted to talk to me—I assumed about the money. We had quite a few drinks and neither of us was particularly sober when I brought the subject up again. He said he didn't have the money on him but he could get it for me quite easily. I agreed to go with him, and he took me to an address in Mount Street, which he told me was his wife's flat. She was very wealthy, he said, and she'd give him whatever he wanted.'

'Did he mention that they were separated?' said Mr. Travers.

'No,' said Valencourt. 'Evidently they didn't live together, but since he let himself in with a key I assumed they were on good terms and that she wouldn't object to his turning up.'

'You did not think it odd that he should bring a friend with him when he went to ask his wife for money?'

'I wasn't thinking about very much at all,' said Valencourt. 'As I said, I'd had rather too much to drink.'

'I see. At what time did you go to the flat?'

'I think it was about a quarter to ten.'

'And what happened when you got there?'

'There was nobody at home, so Marchmont said his wife must be out and that we'd have to wait. I sat down and he said we might as well make ourselves at home and began looking in cupboards for drinks and suchlike. Then he said perhaps she kept some cash lying around in the flat. He looked in the desk drawers but found nothing. After that he went over to the window, opened the top drawer of a little chest there and brought a gun out. He showed it to me and said something like, "Look—this is how much my wife trusts me," and then laughed and put it back. Then he went and stood behind the sofa and looked out of the window, to see if he could see her coming, he said. While he was doing that I went to the chest of drawers and took the revolver from the top drawer out of curiosity.'

'You had no intention of shooting Mr. Marchmont then?'

'None at all, at that point. I just wanted to take a closer look at the gun. Then Marchmont said something or other and I went to join him at the window. I can't remember how the row began, but he made some remark that irritated me, and I snapped back at him. Then he said perhaps he wouldn't pay me after all, and mentioned something that made it perfectly clear he knew the police were looking for me—although I don't know how he found that out, because I certainly didn't tell him. After that he said that perhaps I ought to pay *him* instead for his silence. He had the most insufferable grin on his face when he said it, and I'm afraid I rose to the bait. I said something about how it was unwise to try and blackmail a man with a gun, but he just laughed and said I wouldn't dare. Then he called me a coward and said, "Look, I'm turning my back on you," and practically invited me to do it.' Here he paused. 'So I did,' he said simply.

The silence in court was almost complete as everyone listened, rapt, to Valencourt's story.

'Do you mean you shot him?' said Mr. Travers.

'Yes.'

'At what time was this?'

'Just after ten o'clock, I think.'

'Then what did you do?'

'I left the place in a hurry. I wiped the finger-prints off everything I'd touched, and then went out.'

'Did you lock the door as you left?'

'Yes. Marchmont had left his keys in the lock and I thought it would be better not to arouse suspicion by leaving the door open.'

'What did you do with the keys?'

'I got rid of them somewhere. I can't remember where.'

'And what did you do with the gun?'

'I took it with me.'

'Is this it?' said Mr. Travers, producing a little revolver.

'Yes.'

Mr. Travers turned to the jury. 'Mr. Valencourt handed this gun to me when he came to me on Saturday,' he explained. 'I looked inside it and found that it was almost fully loaded except for one bullet, which was missing. The empty cartridge was still inside. Dr. Menzies has examined the gun and the bullets at my request, and I shall shortly ask him to give evidence to confirm that this is the same gun that was used to kill David Marchmont. In the meantime, I should like to ask Mrs. Marchmont if she can identify this as her gun.'

He handed the revolver to Angela, who looked caught by surprise.

'Mrs. Marchmont, is this your revolver?'

She glanced down at it.

'Yes,' she said after a moment, for it was useless to deny it.

'The one that went missing from your flat?'

She confirmed it with a nod, and Mr. Travers took the gun and turned back to Valencourt.

'Are you acquainted at all with Mrs. Marchmont?' he said.

'No,' replied Valencourt. 'I had only the slightest acquaintance with her husband, and I had no idea he was even married until the night I killed him.'

'Then you have never met her before?'

'No, never.'

'Mr. Valencourt, you are by your own admission a convicted murderer and escaped prisoner, who has successfully eluded capture by the police for ten years or more. Why are you confessing now to the murder of David Marchmont?'

'Because I never intended that anyone else should be blamed for it. I had no idea that his wife would be put on trial for what I did. I may be wicked, but I am not so wicked as to allow someone else to hang for a crime I committed. I killed Mrs. Marchmont's husband, but it was in a moment of anger, and I cannot stand by in cold blood and watch her be tried and convicted of it.'

'Thank you,' said Mr. Travers. 'Now, if you will permit me.'

He turned to Angela.

'Mrs. Marchmont, this man claims he murdered your husband. Did you know anything of this?'

'No,' said Angela with perfect truth.

'And you have never met Mr. Valencourt before?'

Angela opened her mouth to speak. She had been struggling to maintain her composure at this latest turn of events, and had willed herself with every nerve in her body to show no sign of emotion at the awful revelations of the past half an hour. But now all she wanted to do was to speak out, to cry that none of it was true; that Valencourt had told lie after lie under oath; that he barely knew her husband and had had no reason to kill him; that on the contrary he knew *her* very well indeed, and that they had been together on that fateful night before he kissed her goodbye; that she had given him the gun with her very own hands so that he might protect himself from his enemies; that he was confessing to the murder out of some idiotic wish to save her and that it must not be allowed. All this she wanted to say and more. And yet somehow she could not, for everything else was drowned out by those terrible words, *'convicted of the murder of his wife…convicted of the murder of his wife,'* which repeated themselves over and over again in her head with the inexorable rhythm of a drummer drumming some poor soul along the final road to his execution. She had always known he was a thief, but this—this was too much to bear. How could she have been so foolish as to place her trust in him? He was wicked through and through and she wished with all her heart that she had never met him. And yet now she must rely on him to save her.

THE SCANDAL AT 23 MOUNT STREET

Against her will, she found herself looking across the courtroom at Valencourt. He was not looking at her, perhaps to make it easier for her to accept the great favour he had offered her. She hated the obligation under which it would put her, and which would burden her for the rest of her life, but what choice did she have? This was her only way out, and he knew it as well as she did. She turned back to face Mr. Travers. Had she ever met Edgar Valencourt before? That was the question. The court was waiting for her answer and she must give it or die.

'No,' she said firmly at last, and with that one word out of her own mouth damned both him and herself to perdition.

CHAPTER TWENTY-FOUR

A FTER THAT, ANGELA cared not what happened to
her. She withdrew into herself and stared straight ahead
as Dr. Menzies was produced and confirmed, as expected, that
the gun which had been surrendered by Edgar Valencourt was
indeed the one which had been used to kill Davie Marchmont.
Then Jos McLeod was brought back, and identified Valencourt
clearly as the man he had seen threatening Davie on the steps
of Burkett's club on the afternoon of the murder. By this time
the mood in the court had changed palpably from what it
had been only a few days earlier, for now that this dangerous
escaped criminal had come forward to make his extraordi-
nary confession it seemed perfectly obvious to all those in the
public gallery that Angela Marchmont had had nothing to do
with her husband's death, and in fact had very nearly been the
victim of a grave miscarriage of justice.

Sir Benjamin Hicks-Reddington had remained quiet while
all this went on, and had made no move to cross-examine
any of these latest witnesses for the defence. Many took this

as a tacit admission that he had played his hand and lost—for whether he believed Valencourt's story or not, it would surely have looked churlish to insist on pursuing his prosecution of the defendant when there was a perfectly good confession before the court which seemed to fit all the facts neatly enough. Angela Marchmont was generally popular with the public, and her husband had quite obviously been a bad lot whom no-one regretted except his mother, and so Sir Benjamin did not wish to be seen to be responsible for sending her to the gallows if there was any doubt about her guilt. Besides, there would be no damage to his reputation if he let the matter lie, for he had been sure of a win and it was only by pure coincidence that he had been foiled at last.

Mr. Travers, too, was no fool; he was experienced enough to suspect that this sudden confession was perhaps a little too convenient to be true, but was not about to delve too deeply into it, for it answered all his prayers. Whether he believed Angela's assertion that she had never met Edgar Valencourt cannot be said, but he certainly had the good sense not to press the point. He was also careful not to appear to crow, for he saw the way the wind was blowing and had no wish to ruin things at the last minute by provoking his learned colleague into delving too deeply into Valencourt's story. His main concern now was to bring a swift end to proceedings while everybody was still dazzled by the sensational develop-ments of the morning, and to that end he announced that he should like to move for an immediate acquittal if his lordship were quite amenable, since it seemed perfectly evident to him that his client had no case to answer and that she had already suffered quite enough. The judge harrumphed and glanced at the clock, and said it was nearly lunch-time and that the court would adjourn while he considered the matter.

Everybody duly rose and filed out, and Angela was taken to a side room to wait until proceedings recommenced. They had just reached the door of the room in question when the sound of footsteps was heard at the other end of the corridor and Angela glanced up to see Edgar Valencourt, his wrists handcuffed, approaching in company with two policemen. She did not look at him, nor he at her, but the corridor was a narrow one, and as he passed her his step faltered and he turned his head slightly towards her as though he wanted to say something. She looked at the floor. Then one of the policemen gave him a shove and they were gone, and she was left to the pleasure of her own thoughts. It would not be long now. Soon the whole thing would be over and she would know her fate, but for now she would concentrate merely on maintaining her composure. Whatever happened to her, she would never show weakness. She would not allow others to lick their lips at her pain; it should be hers alone.

The judge's luncheon must have been a good one, for when proceedings resumed, after some consultation among all the parties involved, he announced that having reflected on the particularities of the case from all sides, he had concluded that there was quite evidently no need to continue, and without further ado directed the jury to acquit. At that the public gallery burst into cheers, and Freddy and Kathie clutched at one another in relief. There would be various formalities to complete, of course, but Angela was a free woman, acquitted of all charges against her. When the excitement had died down Freddy ran off to submit a triumphant thousand words to the *Clarion* in time for the evening edition, while Kathie hurried to find a telephone box to tell her husband the good news. Sir Benjamin and Mr. Travers shook hands and perhaps exchanged knowing glances, while the public straggled out slowly, all agreeing that the whole thing had been marvellously thrilling and much better than going to the theatre.

Only Angela, standing dazed in the dock, appeared anything less than happy at what had just happened. She had heard the judge's words and knew she ought to be enormously relieved. In reality she felt nothing, for it seemed to her now that her troubles had only just begun and that she was as much alone as ever. On this last point she was wrong, however, for when she finally emerged into the street some time later, expecting to have to seek a taxi, she stopped short as she found William and Marthe waiting patiently with the Bentley to take her home. William opened the door as soon as he saw her and she stepped in. The journey took place in silence, since they all knew it was hardly a moment for celebration—although Angela still had no idea of the part the others had played in her release. There was, of course, no further mention of their dismissal, nor would there be at any other time, for there was no question of their leaving her alone.

When they arrived at Mount Street Angela said nothing but shut herself immediately in her bedroom, got into bed and curled up as tightly as she could under the bedclothes, in a vain attempt to shut out the grief and the pain and the guilt and the self-reproach, which all seemed to scream in her ears at once and threatened to overwhelm her completely. *What had she done?* The thought tormented her, would not let her alone. This was perhaps her lowest moment since the whole thing had begun, and she knew not how to overcome the despair. Sleep: that was what she needed. She had slept little since her arrest, and she knew it had affected her ability to think. She lay quietly, willing sleep to come and take her away from the world, but it was many hours before she at last drifted off, and when she dreamed her dreams were dark ones.

CHAPTER TWENTY-FIVE

ANGELA REMAINED IN bed all that day and half the next. After that, in perhaps as great a feat of strength as she would ever manage, she rose and dressed herself, for she knew she could not hide from the world forever—and besides, there were things to be done. She then emerged from her bedroom and demanded her post, for all the world as though nothing had happened. Marthe had been wringing her hands outside the door since they had got home, and now she fussed about her mistress and urged Madame to eat something, for she must look after herself. Angela was not at all hungry, but she accepted some tea and toast to satisfy Marthe. After she had dealt with the most urgent letters, she summoned Freddy, who presented himself speedily. She waved away his inquiries, and said:

'I understand from Marthe that I have the three of you to thank for my acquittal.'

'Oh, I say,' said Freddy uncomfortably, for he was by no means sure that he had done the right thing, given how it had all turned out.

'You'll forgive me if I don't seem particularly joyful about it,' said Angela. 'All things considered, I think I should have preferred to rely on the goodwill of the jury rather than engage in bare-faced perjury, but please don't suppose for a moment that I'm not grateful for what you did.'

'They'd have found you guilty,' said Freddy. 'You know they would. And we wouldn't be here talking now.'

'Yes,' said Angela. 'Of course I realize that. I only wish—'

She seemed to want to go on, but could not find the words, could not bring herself to mention his name.

'I'm so terribly sorry, Angela,' said Freddy in a rush. 'I had no idea he was going to say what he did. He said you were right not to rely on him for an alibi, but I thought he might have some other evidence he wasn't telling us about. I didn't realize he was going to confess to the whole thing.'

'No, and that is what I wanted to talk to you about. We must find out who killed Davie.'

'What do you mean? We know who killed him.'

'Don't be ridiculous, Freddy,' said Angela. 'Of course he didn't do it. It was all a lie.'

Freddy stared at her in dismay.

'But the gun—'

'I gave him the gun myself on the night of Davie's death. He said he was in danger so I insisted he take it for his own protection. We came back here at a quarter to seven that morning, I gave him the gun and he went away and then I found Davie.'

'But he said he killed Davie at about ten o'clock. He might have done it and then come to the White Rabbit Ball afterwards. It was after eleven when I saw you together.'

'No,' said Angela. 'He didn't know where the gun was kept. He said twice in court that the gun was in the top drawer. But I always kept it in the second drawer. He said it was in the top one because that's where I found it when I gave it to him. I didn't notice at the time, but somebody had obviously put it there by mistake—presumably the killer. Edgar didn't do it, Freddy, I'd swear to it.'

'But then why did he say he did?'

'To save me,' she said.

Freddy regarded her pityingly.

'He's not a good man, Angela,' he said at last.

She turned her head away, but her voice was as steady as ever.

'I know that,' she said. 'I always knew it, although I didn't know quite how bad he was. You don't need to tell me how stupid I've been, because I'm perfectly aware of it. But now that I know everything, I won't be under an obligation to him. We must find out who really killed Davie and bring him to justice.'

'But then they'll know that you lied in court and put you back in prison.'

'That can't be helped,' said Angela. 'My reputation can't get any worse, but at any rate I'm still alive. I have that to thank him for, at least. You will help me, won't you?'

Freddy agreed, and marvelled at Angela's self-possession in the face of what must have been a devastating blow. As for Angela, she had never needed that self-possession more than she did now. She had summoned up all her strength and forced herself to remember that things might have been so much worse, for she might easily have been sent to the gallows for a crime she had not committed. Now she was free. There still remained a wrong that had to be righted, however, and since the law had no interest in doing it she would have to do it herself. There was no hope for Edgar Valencourt; he had committed a dreadful crime and would hang for it, but that had nothing to do with her, and she would not allow him to take another crime upon himself and die in her name. She would find the person who had really killed her husband, inform the police and then retire somewhere to lick her wounds in private—if they would let her. Now she turned her mind to practicalities.

'How did you get on at the White Star offices?' she said.

In all the excitement Freddy had almost completely forgotten his investigations of two weeks earlier. He felt in his pocket for his notebook.

'I did manage to get a list of names out of them,' he said. 'I don't suppose you see anyone you recognize?'

Angela looked at the list and shook her head.

'Davie didn't usually introduce his women to me,' she said. 'Oh dear, it rather looks as though we're back where we started.'

'Never say die,' said Freddy. 'And that's never been truer than now. The *Homeric* is due to dock in three days. I shall go back and speak to my White Star friend and ask him for the address of the first-class steward. If he remembers Davie he might also be able to tell us something of the people he spoke to on board. But Angela, *you're* more likely than anyone else to hold the clue to all this, don't you think? You spoke to him several times before he died. Didn't he say anything to you that seemed odd?'

Angela thought back to the day on which Davie had turned up on her doorstep while she was with Edgar Valencourt. Their conversation had swiftly turned into a row, for even two years apart had not been enough to wear away her resentment at all those years she had wasted as his wife. The argument had followed the same old lines, for after all that time they had nothing new to say to one another. He had brought up the story of Barbara, as he always did, and she had been cowardly enough to cave in to him, as she always did. She frowned. But what else had he said? Something about their not having had children. This was new, surely. It had never seemed to bother him before. Yes—that was it. He had accused her of being frozen, and had said that not all women were like that.

'Were there any women with children on that list?' she said suddenly.

'Not as far as I know,' said Freddy. 'Not unmarried women, at any rate. What is it? You look as though you'd just had a clever idea.'

'I'm not quite sure,' said Angela. 'I just wonder from something Davie said whether there mightn't have been a baby or a child in the picture.' She shook her head impatiently. 'I'm probably imagining things. I dare say he didn't mean anything by it.'

'Well, you knew Davie better than anyone,' said Freddy. 'I shall take your word for it.'

'Still, though,' she said, frowning.

Freddy waited, but she showed no sign of continuing.

'Very well, then,' he said at last. 'I shall root out this mysterious woman—if indeed she exists—and if she knows anything at all about what happened that night you may be sure I'll find it out.'

'Thank you, Freddy,' she said. 'I knew I should be able to rely on you. You've been a good friend to me; don't think I don't know it.'

'Oh, well,' he said, embarrassed. 'Damsels in distress and all that. Mind, I don't say I'll be able to come up with the goods immediately. It might be a while before I can speak to the steward in question—and even then he might not remember much, since it was so long ago.'

'I know you'll do your best,' she said. 'I'd do it myself, but I think I've drawn quite enough attention to myself lately and I should prefer to stay indoors for a while.'

'I quite understand,' said Freddy sympathetically, and took his leave.

Angela sat for a little while, staring into space. Outside, the snow had begun to fall thickly, covering the streets of London with a carpet of white. It would be cold in prison, she thought, and looked towards the crackling fire that Marthe had been tending carefully ever since her return. After a few minutes she found her thoughts drifting in an unwelcome direction, and since she was determined at all costs to suppress her feelings on the subject, she jumped up and began rifling impatiently through cupboards and drawers, in an attempt to keep herself busy and forget what she wanted to forget. She was scrabbling in a little jewellery-box, looking for a missing earring, when she suddenly saw a flash of green and drew in her breath sharply. Heart thumping, she brought out a pretty silver bracelet inlaid with green glass. She stared at it for a long moment. He had given it to her in Venice—to thank her for helping him after he had been shot, he said. She had been reluctant to accept it at first, but after all it was an inexpensive trinket and laid her under no obligation, and so in the end she took it and had worn it for longer than she cared to admit. Now, however, it was nothing but a reminder of terrible things. Her face darkened, and she turned her head and gazed out into the snow.

The next morning, when Marthe came to sweep out the ashes from the fire and lay a new one, she found a twisted lump of blackened metal and glass lying in the grate, and recognized it immediately. Throughout the past few weeks she had remained calm and composed as her mistress stood in the dock, but at the sight of the little bracelet, charred and destroyed, she was overcome and began to weep. As she knelt there sobbing before the fire she felt a hand on her shoulder, almost like a caress, and she turned to see Angela looking down at her, cool and dry-eyed.

'You cry for me, Marthe,' she said. 'I can't.'

She then went away, and Marthe was left to cry all the harder.

CHAPTER TWENTY-SIX

THE SNOW LAY on the ground for more than a week, and so there was no question of venturing outdoors. Angela was glad of it, for she knew she ought to make the effort to get out, but she had been dreading the idea of it, convinced that people would stop and point at her in the street. Far better, she thought, to remain inside where it was warm, and where nobody could see or judge her. The green sofa had been pushed back towards the window, covering the spot where Davie Marchmont had lain, but apart from that, no-one would ever have known that someone had died violently there. Angela was not hypocrite enough to pretend to be sorry at his death, and so the only disturbance she felt at having to remain in the flat was the fact that the new position of the sofa spoilt the symmetry of the room.

On Thursday morning, ten days after her release, Freddy turned up at the Mount Street flat to find Angela reading a newspaper with great attention.

'You've seen it, then,' he said, looking at her carefully.

'If you are referring to the news about Edgar Valencourt, then yes I have,' said Angela, with no more emotion than if they were talking about some new show they had seen.

'Escaped, eh?' said Freddy. 'They ought to have been more careful. They already knew he was a slippery fellow. I don't know why they thought it necessary to move him to another prison. They ought to have known he would make some attempt or other.'

Angela looked up sharply.

'It says here it was an accident—that the prison-van skidded on some ice.'

'Well, yes, that's what it *says*,' conceded Freddy. 'Whether that's what actually happened is another matter altogether.'

'Do you mean you think he arranged the weather deliberately?' said Angela. 'Rather clever of him, if so.'

'Of course not,' said Freddy. 'But you must admit it's been tremendously convenient for him. Why, the man seems to have more lives than a cat.'

He spoke carelessly, but in reality he was watching Angela closely, since he half-suspected that she might know something about it. He might have saved himself the bother, however, for Angela knew nothing and told herself she wanted to know nothing—although she could not prevent herself from reading everything she could about the incident, or wondering where Valencourt was now.

'Still, they'll catch him soon enough,' Freddy went on. 'He can't get far in this weather.'

'I dare say you're right,' said Angela politely. 'Is that why you came, to tell me the news?'

'No,' said Freddy, with some appearance of triumph. 'As a matter of fact, I came to tell you that I've found the girl.'

'Oh,' said Angela in surprise. 'Who is she?'

But she saw that Freddy had no intention of telling her the name without first relating his cleverness in finding it out, and so she listened with every appearance of interest as he told her of what he had been doing for the past week. He had returned to the White Star offices, he said, and had obtained from his friend there the name of the chief steward who had travelled on board the *Homeric* as it carried Davie Marchmont inexorably towards his final destination. Unfortunately, the steward could not remember much about what had happened on that voyage, although he did remember Davie Marchmont very well, given what had happened to him subsequently. Freddy questioned the steward further but got little more out of him, and he was about to give it up when he remembered what Angela had said. Had there been a lady with a child on the ship, he asked. No, there had been no children on board, the steward was sure of that—although he did remember that there had been some talk about one young girl, who was keeping herself well wrapped up but who as far as he could tell was quite obviously expecting. At that, Freddy's ears pricked up and he asked whether the steward could remember her name. The steward racked his brains and at length hazarded that it might have been a foreign name, perhaps Dutch. Van Diemen, possibly? Freddy consulted his notebook, in which he had written the list of women on board. There was a Callie Vandermeer. Might that be she? At that the steward said 'Ah!' and nodded vigorously. She was the one, all right. They had talked about her because she was a Miss, but she had been so sweet and gentle, so polite to all the crew, that nobody had had the heart to be anything other than sympathetic to her plight.

'Where is she now?' said Angela.

'Still here,' said Freddy. 'I looked through all the return passenger lists and asked at the Embassy, but found no trace of her having ever gone back to the United States. That stumped me, rather, until I remembered the baby. It's taken me a week of talking to middle-aged matrons—who to a woman regarded me as the devil incarnate until I managed to convince them that my interest in distressed young ladies was not personal—but this morning I finally got a letter from a place in Whitechapel to say that they have the woman in question and can we please come and get her. I say, Angela, one can't help feeling sorry for these poor girls. Some of these homes for Unspeakable Women are rather awful. It's been a harrowing few days, I don't mind telling you.'

'I imagine it has,' said Angela, who had been fortunate enough to have friends to help her all those years ago. 'Well, if you're sure she's the person we're looking for, then I suppose we had better go and talk to her.'

So it was that Angela and Freddy found themselves on their way to Whitechapel on a freezing January morning, in search of the killer of Davie Marchmont. The Bentley had been rejected as inappropriate, for they did not wish to make themselves conspicuous, and so they took a taxi. It deposited them outside a large, Victorian building in grey stone that seemed designed specifically to intimidate, for inscribed above the door were the words, 'The Lord Hath Chastened Me Sore: But He Hath Not Given Me Over Unto Death.'

'I believe this is meant to be one of the less awful places,' said Freddy, as Angela shivered in the bitter wind and looked about her. He stepped forward and pressed the bell, which was shortly answered by an elderly nun who greeted them kindly and invited them to come in. Inside was barely any warmer than outside, and Angela did not take off her gloves. The nun led them down a long, bare corridor, around which their footsteps echoed loudly, and then into a tiny office, where they were interviewed by another nun—a sterner one this time—and finally escorted up three flights of stairs and into a large room that held ten beds and seemed to serve as a kind of dormitory. Each bed held a woman and an infant, and the noise of crying could be heard from some way away. Freddy averted his eyes as they were led through to one end of the room. Here in a corner was another bed, shut away behind a thin curtain.

'Visitors to see you,' said the stern nun, and pulled the curtain aside. 'You may have half an hour,' she said to Angela and Freddy, as though she intended to throw them out by force if they outstayed their welcome. They thanked her and she left, her footsteps tip-tapping towards the door.

Lying in the bed was a young woman holding a baby. She was pale, and her clothes hung off her as though she had been ill. She looked up at them questioningly.

'Miss Vandermeer?' said Angela.

'Yes?' she replied in a soft American accent. Her eyes were large and brown and her face wore a habitually sweet expression. It was hard to believe that this woman could have killed Davie Marchmont.

'My name is Angela Marchmont,' said Angela. 'I've come to ask you about Davie.'

She looked at them for a moment, and then down at the bed.

'I guess I knew somebody would come eventually,' she said.

CHAPTER TWENTY-SEVEN

IT HAD BEGUN to snow again. The windows of the dormitory were large and high, but they could see the flakes against the grey of the building opposite.

'Are you his wife?' said Callie Vandermeer, looking back up at Angela.

'Yes,' said Angela.

'I'm sorry,' said the girl, and two tears appeared in the corners of her eyes and began to roll down her cheeks. 'I'm so sorry.'

It was impossible to be stiff in the face of such obvious grief. Freddy brought out a handkerchief and handed it to her.

'Thank you,' she said, dabbing her eyes. 'But I don't deserve your kindness, as you can see.' She looked down at the baby, which opened its eyes sleepily and then closed them again. 'He nearly died,' she said. 'And so did I, they tell me. But he's so much stronger now. In a few days, when he's well enough, they'll take him away from me.'

'Shouldn't you rather keep him?' said Freddy.

'I'd like to,' she said. 'But how can I support him, here? I don't have the money to get back home. Davie took care of all that.'

'Don't you have family?' said Angela.

'Only an aunt,' said Callie. 'She'd take me in, but she doesn't have a great deal of money and I'd be too ashamed to ask her to pay for my passage. I'm sorry,' she said again to Angela. 'I'd give anything to go back and do things differently, but I loved him, you see. He said we'd get married and be happy, and I believed him. I guess you were the one to find him. I'm sorry I was such a coward. I know I oughtn't to have left him but I didn't know what to do, and then I got sick and they took me away and brought me here. I only wish I could help in some way, but I don't suppose there's much I can do after all this time. I hope there wasn't too much trouble.'

Her expression was open and innocent, and it was evident she had no idea that Angela had been arrested and put on trial for murder. Angela and Freddy glanced at one another.

'There was a little trouble, yes,' said Angela at last. 'That's why we're here. We want to know exactly what happened that evening. It's rather important.'

Callie looked down and with her free hand smoothed the thin bedclothes.

'All right,' she said. 'But I don't know where to begin.'

'You met Davie in the States, I presume,' said Angela.

'Yes,' said Callie. 'I was in the park and he picked up something I'd dropped, and we got to talking. He was so kind and cheerful that I couldn't help but fall in love with him right away, and he told me he felt the same. I knew pretty quickly that he wasn't—wasn't the best of men, but he mostly treated me well, and I guess I was dazzled by him, and I thought that with a little time and patience he would change. Not long after we met he asked me to marry him and I said yes, and for a little while I was happy, but time went on and he said nothing more about it, and then I found out I was going to have a baby, so I told him we had to get married immediately. It was then that he confessed to me that he was already married. I'd had no idea of it and it came as a horrible shock. He was terribly sorry for what he'd done and said he hadn't meant to lie to me, and that he still wanted to get married, but that he would have to divorce his wife first. He said they'd been living separately for years, and that she was English and had gone back to London, so we'd have to go there and speak to her. He didn't have much money—only just enough to cover the trip there, he said, but his wife was wealthy and would happily agree to a divorce and give him some money too, although it wouldn't be enough for us to live on. Then he laughed and said something about how it didn't matter anyway, because he had another plan in reserve and was minded to carry it out if she wasn't nice to him, and then we'd be set for life. I didn't know what he meant, but he was always saying things I didn't understand and then laughing, and so I thought it was just one of his usual jokes.

'I'd been ill and I didn't want to travel, but he insisted and so I came with him. When we got to London he said that to save money he would go to a friend of his, and he put me in a cheap hotel. For a few days I didn't see very much of him, and spent the days wandering around London by myself—as much as I could, at any rate, because I still wasn't well. By that time I was getting a little fed up with him, to be truthful. I didn't feel he was treating me as he ought, and I made up my mind to tell him so and insist that we go back to New York as soon as possible. So I did, and to my surprise he agreed. He said we'd go back on Sunday and be married immediately on our return, but first he had to carry out his little plan.'

Here she stopped to attend to the child, and Angela and Freddy glanced at one another again. Then Callie looked up.

'I know you must think I'm stupid,' she said. 'I ought to have realized what he meant when he said we'd be married right away. I don't know how long a divorce takes, but I do know it's more than just a few days. But I'd always done what he said, and I trusted him, so I went along with it. On the Saturday night he met me outside the hotel and we went to an apartment in Mayfair. I guess that was yours,' she said to Angela, who nodded. 'He let himself in with a key and we went up to the top floor. It was a little late and I didn't know why he wanted to bring me anyway, because I didn't think you'd be exactly pleased to see me, but he told me to be quiet and that you knew all about me and didn't mind, and that we were going to negotiate a payment. At that point I still had no idea what he was planning, and even when he took the gun out of the drawer I didn't realize what it meant.'

She paused to wipe away the tears, which had started to fall again.

'How could I have been so blind?' she said. 'Mrs. Marchmont, I swear I wouldn't have let him do it. He would have listened to me, I know he would.'

'He was planning to kill Angela,' said Freddy.

Callie nodded.

'There was a life insurance policy,' she said. 'Davie said you'd taken it out years ago when you were first married, and that you'd probably forgotten all about it by now.'

'Yes, I had,' said Angela. 'It was worth rather a lot, as I recall.'

'That's what he said,' said Callie.

The tears were falling freely now, and they waited patiently as she struggled to bring herself under control.

'When I realized what he meant to do I was horrified. I knew he could be a little bad at times, but I had no idea he would resort to murder. I told him I wanted no part of it, and that he'd better let me leave right away. At that he laughed and told me not to be so silly, because I was already a part of it whether I liked it or not, and which would I prefer? To marry him and have a father for the baby and plenty of money, or to be alone and destitute, because that's what I'd certainly be if I insisted on crossing him. At that I said I didn't care about being alone, but I wouldn't be a party to murder and I was going to warn you whatever happened. Then I went to leave, but he stopped me and held the gun to my head and said I was to go nowhere; that I was in with him to the end, and that I was to do what he said. At that I must have started crying, because he became kind again and said he hadn't meant it; that he'd only been joking and he'd never dream of hurting me. Then he started to try and persuade me.' She looked up at Angela. 'He said you were a bad woman and that you had other men and had treated him cruelly. He said that nobody would miss you and that if you died then we would be free. I still couldn't believe it, and I told him so. I said even if he did it, how did he expect to get away with it? The police would know right away that he was the one who'd killed her. Then he laughed and said he had his own insurance policy, and he showed me a glove and said he'd taken it from a man he was pretty sure was your lover. He said he would leave it at the scene of the crime and the man would get the blame and it would serve you both right. He said it would be easy, and started to show me. He went to stand behind the sofa and said, "Look, we'll hide here, and then when she comes in, I'll—I'll—"'

She broke off and gazed at the two of them, her eyes wide and frightened.

'He had the gun in his hand when he was showing me, and his head was turned towards me,' she whispered.

'It went off accidentally,' said Angela.

Callie nodded.

'What time was this?' said Freddy.

'I don't know. Just after ten, maybe. It made the most awful noise. At first I thought he'd done it as a joke, but then I saw he was dead and I knew it was all over. I don't know how long I stood there, but at some point I must have realized that I was going to get into trouble if they found me there. I remember thinking that they'd say I'd killed him, and that I must get away as quickly as possible.'

'Why did you put the gun back in the drawer?' said Angela.

'I don't know, exactly,' said Callie. 'All I know is that I didn't want anybody to guess what Davie had been intending to do. It seemed so important that nobody should find him with the gun in his hand. I felt that it was all my fault, somehow, and that if I'd been a stronger person and had known how to manage him better, then none of it would have happened—

he'd never have dreamed of killing anybody. So I wiped the gun and put it in the drawer, and then I wiped the chest, too, just to be on the safe side, and anything else I could think of. Then I took the keys and locked the door and ran away—I don't know where; I just wandered around London until dawn I think, and then at last I came back to my hotel. I don't really remember much about what happened after that, but they tell me I collapsed and was ill for quite a while. Then they brought me here.'

She looked down at the baby.

'They say it was touch and go for a few weeks, but they think he'll do well now that he's over the worst,' she said. 'I wanted to call him David, but I don't know if it's such a good idea—and anyway there doesn't seem much sense in giving him a name if I won't get to keep him.'

She fell silent, then. The baby gave a little murmur and she caressed its head.

Angela regarded the poor girl before her, who had been fooled and betrayed in love, and who had unwittingly brought about such misery, and felt nothing but pity.

'Will you sign a written statement of what you've just told us?' said Freddy.

'I guess I will,' said Callie. 'It's only right. Am I going to get into trouble?'

'No,' said Freddy. 'It's just a formality, so that no-one else can be blamed for it.'

'All right,' said Callie. 'Will you write it for me? I'm not very strong yet.'

'Of course,' said Freddy.

'Oh,' she said suddenly. 'I still have the keys. You'd better take them.'

She indicated a little box on the floor by the bed. Freddy looked through the pitifully few possessions that lay inside it and brought out a set of keys. He handed them to Angela, who put them in her pocket.

'I know the two of you were separated,' said Callie, 'and I know he wasn't a good man, but I'd like you to know that I'm truly sorry for what happened. I never got to be his wife, so I guess I don't matter so much—'

She could not go on, for the tears had begun rolling down her cheeks again.

Angela could bear it no longer. She came to a decision.

'Where shall you go when you leave here?' she said.

'I don't know,' said Callie, drying her tears. 'Maybe I'll look for domestic work. I want to pay my passage back to America as soon as I can. I don't know how long it will take, though.'

She looked wistfully at the baby and stroked its head.

'You needn't worry about that,' said Angela. 'It can all be arranged, but you must get well first. This place is hardly conducive to good health. We must find somewhere more comfortable for you and the baby, and when you're both quite well again we'll see about sending you home.'

Callie's eyes widened in wonder.

'Do you really mean that?'

'Of course I do. You've had rather a rotten time of it, all told, and I think the best thing will be to get you home as soon as possible,' said Angela.

Callie began to stammer out her thanks, but Angela waved them away.

'There must be lots of comfortable nursing-homes here in London,' she went on briskly. 'I'm sure we can find one that will take you and the baby.'

'Then I may keep him?' said Callie. 'I'd like to.'

'Do,' said Angela. 'He's your son, after all. Call him David, as you wanted to, and bring him up to be a better man than his father was.'

They bade Callie Vandermeer goodbye and promised that she should be moved that very day, if possible. Then they left the building and stepped out into the swirling snow of Whitechapel.

CHAPTER TWENTY-EIGHT

'I DON'T KNOW what he was thinking,' said Angela when they were safely back at Mount Street. 'I'd written him a cheque only a few days earlier, and that would have led the police straight to him. I don't know why he thought they'd care about an odd glove when they had a perfectly good suspect right in front of their eyes. Why, it would have taken them no time at all to dig up that old insurance policy.'

'Was it a large one?' said Freddy.

'A hundred thousand dollars,' said Angela, and Freddy whistled. 'As I recall, it was his idea,' she went on dryly. 'Rather stupid of me to forget about it, though.'

'But why did Davie ask you for money when he was already planning to kill you?' said Freddy.

'Pure greed, I imagine,' said Angela. 'He knew I'd pay up—I always did. I suppose he thought of it as pocket-money to keep him going until he got the grand prize. Idiotic of him, though. One might say it was his bad luck that the gun went off before he could kill me, but if it hadn't, then he'd certainly have done it and been caught and hanged anyway.'

'How did he know where to find the gun, by the way?'

'He was rummaging around in that chest of drawers the first day he turned up,' said Angela. 'I expect he saw it then. And when Callie was cleaning up after he shot himself, she must have put it back in the wrong drawer. I ought to have kept the thing locked up. I won't be so careless again.'

'Well, I know one's not supposed to speak badly of the dead, but I'll make an exception in his case,' said Freddy. 'Good riddance to him, I say. If anyone deserved to be hoist with his own petard, he did. That idea of pinning your murder on Valencourt was particularly ill-natured. I wondered what he meant by that remark about throwing down the gauntlet, and now we know. I dare say he thought he was being tremendously witty when he said it.'

'I dare say he did,' said Angela. 'He always liked to laugh at his own jokes, even when they weren't particularly funny.'

'It's just *your* bad luck that you were the one to find him,' said Freddy. 'If you hadn't been then you might never have been arrested in the first place.'

'Yes,' said Angela bitterly. 'Funny, isn't it? In effect I was put on trial for what was intended to be my own murder. It's not exactly what Davie planned, but I'm quite sure he would have laughed about it for days if he'd known.'

They fell silent, for the wound was still fresh.

'You're not really going to tell the police the truth about Edgar Valencourt, are you?' said Freddy at length.

'Of course I am,' said Angela.

'But what good will it do?'

'It will clear his name,' said Angela. 'I want everybody to know who really killed Davie. I want the police to know it, and the judge to know it, and I want to read it in the newspapers, and I want people in the street to talk about it. Justice has not been done, and I want it to be done.'

'But then they'll want to know why Valencourt confessed,' said Freddy. 'And then it will come out that you knew him and lied in court about it, and then the whole thing will begin all over again.'

'I know,' said Angela. 'But somehow I'd rather that than suffer this burden of obligation. I won't have it, I tell you. I never asked him to do what he did, and since there's nothing I can do about his past crimes then the least I can do is clear him of this one.'

'But it won't do any good,' said Freddy. 'And besides, he's gone on the run again so they won't be hanging him for the present anyway. At least you won't have that on your conscience. Look here, Angela, I know you've had a hard time of it, but I want you to listen to me as a friend. Don't say anything to the police, or to anyone. Valencourt is a bad lot who deserves everything he gets, but it appears that he does have *some* finer feelings at least. Look at what he did for you. If he hadn't said what he did in court then they'd never have acquitted you and we might never have found Callie Vandermeer. It can never make up for what he did to his wife, of course, but don't forget that he needn't have come forward at all. He might easily have refused to come back with us, but he didn't. He must think an awful lot of you to have given himself up.'

Angela opened her mouth to object, but Freddy went on:

'Let it lie for now. Let him do you this favour. He's disap-peared anyway, so what purpose can it possibly serve to open Pandora's box again? Why, none at all. You'll probably be ar-rested for perjury and Valencourt will still be free, and all his efforts will have gone to waste. We have Callie's statement, and now that we know where she is we can call upon her if needs be. Keep your secret. Save it at least until he's been recaptured. He doesn't need your help now.'

'But it will all come out sooner or later anyway,' said Angela. 'Lots of people in Italy know I knew him. He was using an alias but eventually someone will put two and two together and realize the truth.'

'But why should they, if he was using an alias? And even if they do, and decide to report it to the police, then you're still no worse off than you would have been if you'd gone to the police yourself. They can't try you again for murder, and we know now that it wasn't murder anyway. Think how dis-appointed Jameson will be in you, too. He'll never let you do any detecting again.'

'I have no intention of ever doing any detecting again anyway,' said Angela. 'Not after what's happened. How would it look, do you suppose, for a woman who was once charged with murder herself, and who got off by lying in court, to go around claiming to represent justice? I couldn't possibly do it; my conscience won't allow it.'

'That's a pity,' said Freddy. 'You're rather good at it. Scotland Yard will be terribly upset.'

'I'm quite sure Scotland Yard will breathe a sigh of relief when they find out they won't have to put up with my meddling ever again,' said Angela. 'And once they know about what I did then they won't let me anyway.'

'I'm sorry all this had to happen,' said Freddy. 'It's been the most awfully foul time for you, I know, and I quite understand why you want to put things right, but do keep quiet, Angela, for Barbara's sake at least. How do you think she's going to feel about it all?'

That brought her up short. Of course Angela was not the only person to have been affected by the trial. Barbara was still in India with the Ellises, but they would be back soon and it would all have to come out—if indeed it had not already. Barbara was quite sharp-witted enough to have realized that something was going on and to have found out what it was, and Angela quailed at the thought of the conversation which would inevitably follow.

'I don't suppose she'll ever speak to me again,' she said. 'But I expect you're right. Having a mother in prison is hardly going to do much for her school-work, is it? And she'd been doing rather well lately.'

She paused. Freddy was right, of course. If she wanted to put things right with Barbara then the sensible thing would be to say nothing at present. The law was satisfied that justice had been done, and the only reason to disabuse it of that notion while Valencourt was still at large would be to assuage her own feelings of guilt. Heaven knew she had had plenty of practice at living with a guilty conscience, so what difference could it possibly make?

'Very well, then,' she said. 'I shall keep quiet about it for the moment.'

'Splendid,' said Freddy. 'Then that's settled. You'll say nothing to the police, we'll keep Callie's statement somewhere safe, and Marthe and William and I will forget we ever knew anything to your disadvantage—at least until Valencourt is recaptured.'

'And then you'll let me go to the police?'

'No, then I'll come and talk you out of it again,' said Freddy. 'I refuse to let you punish yourself for something that wasn't your fault. You're a good woman, Angela, and you're much better off out of prison than in. I won't say the law is an ass, but it very nearly was in this case, and I'd say that you were perfectly justified in doing what you did.'

Angela said nothing, but she could not agree that the question was quite so black and white as Freddy painted it. She had denied having ever met Edgar Valencourt in order to save herself, and in so doing had condemned him to the harshest of all penalties. No matter that the same penalty already awaited him for another crime; no matter that he had invited her to do it as clearly as if he had spoken the words; what she had done was wrong, and she knew that she would not be able to live with herself until she had confessed all to the police. Perhaps he had done it for love of her, but she did not want that sort of love, for it was nothing but a poisoned chalice and a reminder of everything she hated about herself at present. She would keep quiet for Barbara's sake, but only as long as Valencourt remained free. As soon as he was recaptured, however, she would go to the police and right the wrong she had done him. He should not be allowed to die with her sins upon his head, she was quite determined. He was a bad man, and she would repay the debt she owed him, then leave him to his fate and do her best to forget him.

CHAPTER TWENTY-NINE

IT WAS A cold, damp day in early February. The snow had mostly melted; only little banks of it remained here and there, and the garden looked bleak as Angela stepped out of the Ellises' house and onto the terrace. There was a little wooden shelter with a bench halfway down the lawn—not exactly a summer-house, for it was open at one side, but it was dry at least. Barbara was sitting on the bench, watching a robin as it hopped about in a nearby tree. She looked up as Angela joined her. She was very brown from her time abroad.

'May I sit down?' said Angela.

Barbara moved along a little to make room.

'How did you like India?' said Angela.

'It was all right, I suppose,' said Barbara. 'Fearfully hot, of course. I was nearly bitten by a snake.'

'Dear me,' said Angela.

'The fellow said it was a good thing it didn't get me, because my arm would have swelled up like a balloon and they'd have had to amputate to stop the venom going to my heart and killing me.'

'Goodness,' said Angela. 'Why did it go for you?'

'Oh, because I tried to pick it up, I expect,' said Barbara. 'Gerald gave me the most awful wigging.'

'I'm not surprised,' said Angela.

There was a pause. They both stared straight ahead.

'I see you got off, then,' said Barbara at length.

'Yes,' said Angela.

'Your husband sounds like he was an ass. Good riddance to him, I say.'

'Er—' said Angela, unsure as to whether she ought to agree or not. She knew vaguely that one ought not to encourage children to show disrespect to their elders or to the dead, but on the other hand she was fairly sure that one ought also to teach them to speak the truth. She struggled with this for a second and then gave it up.

'Well, I didn't do it, of course,' she said, 'so they had to release me in the end.'

'Yes, I read all about it in the newspapers,' said Barbara.

'I hoped you wouldn't,' said Angela. 'I thought Nina would keep you from seeing them.'

'She tried, but I sneaked out and bought them whenever I could. I had the right to know what was going on, didn't I?'

'We didn't want you to be upset,' said Angela.

'But why?' said Barbara. 'I'm not a child any more. I'm four-teen now. That's practically grown-up.'

Angela looked sideways at her. Could this really be the tiny child she had given up all those years ago? She had grown so tall and strong, so stout-hearted and so determined, and she had become all this despite never having known her parents. Perhaps she had never needed Angela at all—never would need her. What could a mother offer her, now, that she could not provide for herself? Angela drew a deep breath. The subject could no longer be avoided.

'If you were reading the papers—' she began, then stopped, for she could not bring herself to go on. How to say it?

Barbara came to her rescue.

'I expect you're talking about what that woman said in court,' she said as carelessly as possible.

'Yes,' said Angela. 'Have Nina and Gerald mentioned anything?'

'No. They said better to wait for you.'

'Oh,' said Angela. It was cowardly of her, she knew, but she had half-hoped that the Ellises would have talked it all out with Barbara by the time she arrived so that she would be spared the necessity of explaining and excusing herself.

'Is it true?' said Barbara.

'Yes,' said Angela, and found that it was not as hard to say as she had expected. 'I'm sorry I didn't tell you before.'

'Why didn't you?'

'Because for a long time I thought you were better off not knowing,' said Angela. 'I wasn't married to your father, you see, and I thought you'd be happier if you never knew that. People can be rather tiresome about that sort of thing, and I didn't want you to have to suffer cruel remarks about it.'

'Were you ashamed of me?' said Barbara. She was fiddling with her wrist-watch and not looking at Angela.

'No!' said Angela quickly. 'I was never ashamed of you—only of myself. I should have liked so much to have kept you with me, but it would have been very hard on you to grow up without a father, and Nina and Gerald were so kind to me and so keen to have you that it seemed the best thing to do. Then I married Davie, and—' here she could not bring herself to say, '—and he didn't want you,' so she went on hurriedly, '—and then when I came back to England and you were growing up, somehow I couldn't tell you then, either. You'll come into quite a lot of money one day, you see, and I wanted you to have all sorts of nice things—a proper coming-out, and the chance to wear pretty dresses and meet nice young men and marry one of them without people whispering behind their hands and sneering about it.'

'But I don't care about things like that,' said Barbara in surprise.

'Not now, but you will one day,' said Angela. She looked down at her gloves. 'I always meant to tell you sooner or later—truly I did, but somehow it never seemed quite the right time, and the longer it went on the more difficult it became. But it was all for nothing anyway,' she went on bitterly, 'because everybody knows about it now. The whole country, in fact. I'm so terribly sorry, Barbara. I certainly never meant this to happen. I'd give anything for you not to have been dragged into it.'

Barbara did not reply, but picked industriously at a finger-nail.

'Did you love him?' she said at length. 'My father, I mean.'

'Yes,' said Angela. 'Very much. We were to be married, but he died shortly before the wedding. For a long time I thought I should never get over it.'

'Nina would never tell me much about him,' said Barbara. 'I know he was her brother, of course, but she said there was no sense in talking about the past when it couldn't bring him back. And she wouldn't say a thing about my mother, except to say that she was dead. I thought perhaps she hadn't liked her much, but now I see why.'

'Nina and Gerald have been good friends to me. To us both,' said Angela. 'I can never repay them for what they've done. And you've been happy with them, haven't you?'

She asked this anxiously. She knew she had not been a good mother, but she had sincerely wanted Barbara to be happy and had done her best to ensure that she would have a comfortable life with Jack's family.

'Yes, I suppose so,' said Barbara. 'They've been jolly decent, really. I mean, I know I'm troublesome and all that—'

'No you're not,' said Angela. 'I know they're very proud of you and think of you quite as their own.'

'But I'm not, am I?' said Barbara. 'I'm yours. Or I ought to be, at least.'

This could not be denied, and Angela knew not what to say. They were silent for some minutes, watching the robin as it busied itself about in the garden, then Barbara went on, still in that careless tone:

'I used to wonder about my mother quite often when I was very young. I'd try to imagine what she was like, but it was difficult when I didn't have even a photograph and when nobody would tell me anything about her.'

'How did you imagine her to be?' said Angela.

'Kind, mostly,' said Barbara. 'I thought she'd be kind, and not be too cross about things like mud on the carpets and jam in my hair. Nina gets terribly annoyed about things like that.'

'Yes, I expect she does,' said Angela.

'Then for a while I had the idea that perhaps she was still alive, and I used to stare at anyone who visited and wonder whether she was really my mother, and whether everyone was keeping it from me. But I got into trouble for staring so I had to stop.'

She was now squinting very hard at the top branches of a nearby sycamore tree.

'Of course, I stopped wishing years ago,' she went on. She hesitated, and then said, half-unwillingly, with a brief glance at Angela, 'But then you came, and I'd only ever had letters from you before, and they said you'd returned from America for good, and you were such a sport whenever we met, that—' she broke off. 'Perhaps I did wish, then,' she said. 'Just a little bit.'

'I wished too,' said Angela quietly.

'Did you?' said Barbara, looking at Angela properly for the first time. 'What did you wish for?'

'Lots of things. Mostly I wished that Jack hadn't died, and that I hadn't had to give you to someone else, and that we could have all been happy together as a family.'

'I'd have liked that,' said Barbara. 'Perhaps I wouldn't have kept getting into trouble as I do now.'

'Perhaps,' said Angela, with a small smile. 'It is a dreadful pity Jack's not here. He'd have known how to manage you. How to manage us both, in fact.'

'I didn't think you needed managing,' said Barbara. 'I thought you were supposed to be awfully capable.'

'Sometimes I wonder,' said Angela. 'I don't seem to have made a terribly good fist of things lately.'

She hesitated, wondering whether she had any right to ask the question, and how she would feel if Barbara wanted nothing more to do with her. After all, the girl had every right to be angry at what had happened.

'Look here,' she said at length, 'I'll quite understand if you want to say no, but I'd like to be your mother now, if you'll have me.'

Barbara looked up, and Angela, feeling rather an idiot, went on:

'I don't say I know much about it—quite the contrary, in fact. Nina's much better at that sort of thing than I am—'

'No she's not,' said Barbara quickly. 'She couldn't possibly be.'

'Well, I'm willing to try,' said Angela. 'If you'll have me,' she added again.

'Of course I will,' said Barbara.

'Good. Then that's settled,' said Angela, although quite *what* was settled she was not entirely certain. Truth to tell, she was not a little concerned that Barbara might propose moving in with her at Mount Street there and then, and she felt some trepidation at the thought of what that might entail. What did children eat, exactly? Fortunately, Barbara had more sense and experience in such matters than Angela did.

'I suppose you'll want me to stay at school,' she said.

'Oh, naturally,' said Angela. 'But you can come to me in the holidays.'

'But what about Nina and Gerald?' said Barbara. 'I'm very fond of them, of course. I shouldn't like to desert them. Perhaps you could share me.'

'Well, I dare say we can come to an agreement,' said Angela with a sense of relief that she would never have admitted. She would not, after all, have to learn how to be a mother to a fourteen-year-old girl all at once. The Ellises would help her as they always had, and she could learn it all gradually.

There was an uncomfortable silence which threatened to become downright embarrassing. Then Barbara jumped up.

'I say, come and see the den Tom and I made last summer,' she said. 'I think there are rats living in it.'

'How splendid,' said Angela, who was not fond of rats.

She stood up and they made their way across the garden, and they spent some time poking about. Barbara was chattering away about what she intended to do once she got back to school, and Angela was glad of the distraction, for she had spent too much time alone with her own thoughts lately. The question of whether she ought to go to the police had unexpectedly resolved itself a week ago, when news had come that Edgar Valencourt had been shot and killed in Paris. He had evaded the police easily enough, but could not escape his enemies, it seemed. A number of witnesses had seen the altercation, heard the gunshot, seen the body fall into the Seine, and there was no doubt, therefore, of what had happened. His body had been recovered some days later and identified by a relation of his, and the newspapers were full of congratulatory stories about his demise. Angela had read the news, apparently unmoved, and when Freddy had called to see how she had taken it, had assured him that she felt nothing. It was what he deserved, she said, and she was only pleased that it had happened this way, for at least now she should never have his hanging upon her conscience. Whether Freddy believed her or not cannot be said, but her self-possession was by now complete and she would never admit weakness, and so he was forced to be content with that.

It was getting colder now, and the thought of a warm fire was inviting, so they turned and began to walk slowly towards the house.

'I wonder what I've missed at school,' said Barbara. 'Violet says that Miss Bell has saved up two months' worth of maths prep for me. I hope she was joking.'

'You'll have to catch up,' said Angela, feeling a pang of guilt at the work Barbara had been forced to miss.

'Oh, I'm sure I shall,' said Barbara carelessly.

'I hope there won't be too much teasing about—' said Angela hesitantly.

'About you, you mean? Don't worry, if there is I'll know what to do about it.'

'I hope you don't mean to get into trouble,' said Angela.

'Of course not,' said Barbara. 'Do you think I'm stupid enough to do it in front of the mistresses?' She saw Angela's look of alarm and grinned. 'I was only joking,' she said. 'I dare say the Everard female will be a pig, but I'm used to that. I just ignore her these days. I had a very kind letter from Mam'selle, by the way. She didn't say anything about it, but I'm sure all the teachers know.'

'Mam'selle has known for a while,' said Angela. 'She guessed when I was there in October.'

'Did she?' said Barbara in surprise. 'However did she do that?'

'I dare say she thinks we look alike,' said Angela.

'Really? I can't see it myself, although people do persist in thinking you're my aunt. I wonder if that's the reason.'

'I suppose it might be,' said Angela. She was thinking of Callie Vandermeer, who had at last returned to America with her baby. Callie had not been so fortunate as Angela, who had had friends and money to help her through her trouble fourteen years ago, and yet she at least had kept her child in the end, while Angela had felt forced to let hers go. What an irony it was that it had been Angela herself who had found Callie and rescued her. And what a pity that Callie had been unable to influence Davie quite enough to prevent him from doing what he had done, for had he been a little less obstinate, there was no saying that she might not have been the making of him in the end, since it seemed to Angela that Davie had had a genuine affection for the girl. As it was, Callie had been left with nothing but a broken heart and a hungry mouth to feed. Still, she was back with her family now, and it was to be hoped that she and the baby would do well.

They stopped by a pond and peered into its muddy depths. Having succeeded in quashing all uncomfortable thoughts that morning in her worry about the difficult conversation that had lain ahead of her, Angela was now more than a little disconcerted when Barbara suddenly said:

'I *am* glad they found out who really did it in the end, and let you go. But don't you think it's the oddest thing that Edgar Valencourt, of all people, should have turned out to be the murderer? I mean, it's the most tremendous coincidence.'

Angela glanced up sharply, but Barbara was poking at a bank of muddy snow with a stick, quite unconscious of having said anything remarkable. Angela had feared that she would put two and two together, but it appeared that she was still innocent enough to believe what she had been told. One day, perhaps, she would realize that there was more to the story than met the eye, but for now it looked as though Angela were safe.

'Yes, I suppose it is a coincidence,' she said.

'I'm sorry he turned out to be a murderer,' went on Barbara. 'I mean to say, I know he was a thief, but I should never have thought of him as the violent type when we met him that time in Cornwall. As a matter of fact, I rather liked him.'

She bent over to tie her shoelace, which had come loose.

'So did I,' said Angela after a moment, so softly that Barbara did not hear her.

Barbara straightened up.

'You're looking a bit peaky, Angela,' she said. 'I don't suppose it was much fun being in gaol. Perhaps you ought to go away for a week or two.'

'Perhaps I shall,' said Angela.

And perhaps she would. She had had an invitation only that morning from some friends of hers who were sympathetic to her plight, and who wanted her to come with them to the South of France. The weather would be warm and there would be lots of friendly people and it would all be very gay, they promised her. It sounded very appealing, for anywhere would be better than here at present, and she did not want to be alone.

'You will come back though, won't you?' said Barbara, and there was a little note of anxiety in her voice. 'You're not going to run off again, I hope.'

'Of course I'll come back,' said Angela. 'You won't get rid of me now. Just you wait and see.'

'Good,' said Barbara. She shivered. 'I'm cold. Let's go and have some tea.'

For a few seconds they stood facing one another, and at that moment no-one could have doubted the resemblance between them. They had spent so many years apart, and who knew whether what had been lost could ever be recovered? Still, now was the time to try. There was a pause as they gazed uncertainly at one another, then Barbara smiled and linked her arm through Angela's, and mother and daughter turned and walked back towards the warmth of the house.

New Releases

If you'd like to receive news of further releases by Clara Benson, you can sign up to my mailing list here: clarabenson.com/newsletter.

Books in This Series

- The Murder at Sissingham Hall
- The Mystery at Underwood House
- The Treasure at Poldarrow Point
- The Riddle at Gipsy's Mile
- The Incident at Fives Castle
- The Imbroglio at the Villa Pozzi
- The Problem at Two Tithes
- The Trouble at Wakeley Court
- The Scandal at 23 Mount Street
- The Shadow at Greystone Chase

Also by Clara Benson:
The Freddy Pilkington-Soames Adventures